Praise for *Bear Se[...]*

'Bloody hell! *Bear Season* is terrific. A supremely confident blend of found-footage, true crime, and dark fairy tales that I found utterly impossible to put down. Fairclough's debut refuses easy answers and categorisation, just like the two women who become entangled in this dark story about a missing British PhD student in the Alaskan wilderness. Simply addictive.'
– Ally Wilkes, author of *All the White Spaces*

'Mystery and longing intertwine seductively in this compelling exploration of three women's minds. All three are drawn inexorably to the Alaskan forest, where desire, grief and fear take on wilder forms, and human nature might blur with animal instinct. *Bear Season* asks: what does each of us conceal, under our pelts?'
– Zoe Gilbert, author of *Folk* and *Mischief Acts*

'*Bear Season* is a deft, thoughtful, unique gem of a book. Crafted with care, skill and sensitivity, it weaves together tension, mystery, ambiguity and obsession, questioning the stories we live and tell, and exploring the unanswered questions and legacies that we leave behind. Innovative, atmospheric and unsettling.'
– Jane Claire Bradley, author of *Dear Neighbour*

First published in 2024 by Wild Hunt Books
wildhuntbooks.co.uk

Copyright © 2024 by Gemma Fairclough

Gemma Fairclough has asserted her right to be identified as the
author of this Work in accordance with the Copyright, Design
and Patents Act 1988

A CIP catalogue record for this title is available from the British Library

Paperback: 978-1-7394580-0-3
Ebook: 978-1-7394580-1-0

Typeset by Laura Jones-Rivera
Cover Design by Luísa Dias
Edited by Ariell Cacciola

BEAR SEASON

On the Disappearance of Jade Hunter
by Carla G Young

GEMMA FAIRCLOUGH

WILD
HUNT
BOOKS

Preface

In this thesis, part academic inquiry, part fairy tale and vision quest, I document a journey to Bear, whose teeth and claws will tear away the skin of this life, whose jaws are a gateway to the next.

So commences the document entitled 'Thesis' emailed by twenty-five-year-old student Jade Hunter to her PhD supervisor five days before she was reported missing on April 15, 2016.

The day before this email with the attached 'Thesis' was sent, Jade began her seven-thousand-mile journey from Manchester, England, to attend the Global Symposium on Fairy Tales, Fables and Folklore, a biennial academic conference hosted in 2016 at the University of Alaska Fairbanks (UAF). After four connecting flights and a cab ride from Fairbanks International Airport, she arrived in College, a suburb of Fairbanks – one of the very few blemishes of urbanisation upon Interior Alaska's wild beauty. It was a far cry from the vibrant industrial city where Jade lived: Manchester, a place with a pulse, thronging with students and sound. During a trip to England, I'd spent a week in Manchester exactly one year before Jade's disappearance; I might have passed her in the street. As for College, I lived there briefly in 1997 before moving back to my hometown of Portland, Oregon. I remember being struck by news coverage of the missing woman: both she and I had traversed two points on the world map that had very little to do with one other. That was the first of several coincidences that would arise in my relationship to this case.

Jade's journey to Alaska was a significant undertaking for a five-day conference, her partner and father agreed (one of very few matters they saw eye to eye). What they hadn't known was that Jade had bought a one-way ticket. She hadn't planned on coming back.

Local authorities were first alerted to Jade's disappearance by her partner, a thirty-nine-year-old activist named Otto Lock, who told police he had expected Jade to contact him on the night of her arrival to let him know she'd reached her hotel safely. Nor had she answered his dozens of calls and messages in the days that followed. Police investigations began at the UAF campus. Witness statements concerning the missing woman conflicted: one witness, a delegate at the conference, claimed to have seen the young British student on the first day of the programme, Monday, April 11. However, the conference organisers reported that Jade never showed up for registration and was noted absent. Several other witnesses on campus and at a nearby hotel, where Jade checked in on Sunday, April 10, and where several other delegates were staying, reported having seen Jade between April 10 and 11 but admitted that their recollections of the days and times of these sightings were hazy. College is one of very few places in Interior Alaska that may be described as liberal; furthermore, everyone who attends an arts and humanities academic conference almost anywhere in the world can expect a free wine reception. One can imagine the state troopers' frustration as they tried to tease out specific details of their witnesses' drink-addled memories.

The last known sighting of Jade was on the afternoon of April 11, reported by a gas station clerk who saw a woman of Jade's description walking alone past the gas station on the outskirts of town, fifteen miles away from the UAF campus. Search and rescue operations began in College and moved through Fairbanks and the surrounding area, but no evidence of Jade's whereabouts was found for the first two weeks. Criminology experts agree that the first seventy-two hours investigating a missing person case are the most critical; beyond that, leads wane, evidence gets lost in a series of dead ends, the case goes cold.

Then, on May 1, police were called to a remote area beyond the city limits – a woman had opened fire at two Alaska State Troopers as they drove up the road towards her home. The troopers had been investigating the missing person case and were patrolling the area. One bullet burst through the car windshield and hit Sergeant Paul Mathers between the eyes, killing him instantly. Covered in his supervisor's blood and brains, Trooper Frank Sweeney, star graduate of the Alaska State Trooper Academy training programme, calmly called for backup, then got out of the vehicle and fired his weapon. Sweeney performed what was later described by his division as "a selfless act of mercy"[1] and earned him a Real Heroes Award from the American Red Cross of Alaska: rather than killing his assailant, he only disarmed her by shooting her in the leg. Sweeney survived the incident unscathed, while the woman was treated for minor injuries in hospital before being taken into custody.

At first, the shooting appeared to be a random act of violence and an all-too-familiar tragedy in the USA; Alaska has the highest rate of gun ownership of any state in the country. But as investigations into the killing of the trooper continued, so grew the complexity of the case.

The unkempt, jabbering woman taken into custody was hard to pin down. Eventually identified as sixty-two-year-old Ursula Smith by medical records from her childhood – she had no known birth certificate – she refused to talk to the police and offered no justification or defence of her actions. A psychiatric evaluation – quoted by Ursula's defence attorney during the trial the following year – found that, rather than remorseless, Ursula was fearful of the police. The evaluation

---

1 "Woman taken into custody following officer-involved shootout in Fairbanks." *Fairbanks Daily News-Miner,* May 2, 2016. While the Alaska State Troopers' official stance was outright praise for Sweeney's actions, a more ambivalent view was offered a year later by former (and the only female) Fairbanks Police Department detective Kate Whittle, who briefly mentioned the incident when speaking to the press following her resignation: "I had real concerns about how [Mathers and Sweeney] handled that investigation, how they targeted [Ursula] in the first place. There's a lot of sexism going on in law enforcement in Alaska, a lot of intimidation of female civilians and officers. I speak from personal experience." See "Fairbanks detective alleges sexist culture in resignation." *AP News,* November 29, 2017.

noted that she was "paranoid about stating anything on record that she believed might be used to incriminate her further."[2]

Police conducted a search of Ursula's property. Behind the log cabin, alongside a vegetable patch and a well – drilled without a permit, they soon ascertained – they observed solar panels and a shed housing a backup generator; the cabin had no mains electricity supply. One of the cabin windows was broken. Inside the cabin, among taxidermied animals and a rack with a formidable collection of firearms, was a tower of dusty boxes containing Ursula's journals; excerpts from these would be read aloud in the trial months later. Police found no phone, computer, or TV – none of the apparatus of modern life. They confirmed that Ursula was a fur trapper by trade; in the workroom, lynx and fox furs were piled up, ready for sale. Here was the worktable – its wood grain bloodstained, officers noted – where she expertly extracted her wares, cleared and ready for its next use. On a rack above were knives of various shapes and sizes for all manner of cutting. Rotting in a pot on the stove were remnants of a meal of stewed meat. What Ursula didn't eat from her hunts, she buried; later, police would dig up scores of graves – unearthing bone fragments as well as complete skeletons – surrounding the cabin in concentric circles, a pattern that would be described by Ursula's prosecutors as "ritualistic."[3]

Ursula captured the attention of the media and the public imagination. Local and even national TV news sta-

2 See transcripts from court proceedings on the Alaska Trial Court Cases index, *Ursula Smith v State of Alaska*.
3 Ibid.

tions broadcasted long, in-depth reports on the shootout – interrupted occasionally by brief updates on the ongoing search for the missing young woman, Jade Hunter – speculating about the circumstances that had led Ursula to kill forty-four-year-old Sgt. Mathers. As more information about Ursula's background came to light, various reporters described Ursula as a "crazed libertarian" and "reclusive survivalist," quoting unnamed sources postulating that she was a "textbook paranoid schizophrenic" with a "lifelong fear of the police." Perhaps because the story coincided with updates on the increasingly hopeless search for the missing woman, last seen twenty miles away from Ursula's home, other suspicions gradually arose. Indicted for one murder already – the killing of Mathers – could Ursula have also had a hand in Jade's disappearance?

On May 17, another search of Ursula's cabin led to a turning point: in one of the bedrooms, a torn piece of paper was discovered under the bed. Written on in cramped, ink-blotted scrawl – later analysed and confirmed by a graphologist to resemble Jade's handwriting – it read:

She's locked me in. She won't let me go.

While Jade's narrow handwriting appears constricted, inhibited, Ursula's handwriting is large and loud, written in all caps. It wobbles off the lines. It gobbles up the page.

During the trial, a page taken from one of Ursula's journals was projected onto a screen while the prosecutor read it aloud. The jury studied the page, shifting in their seats uneasily as they listened:

THE GOVERNMENT DON'T WANT YOU TO KNOW THE END IS COMING. THEY WILL DO ANYTHING TO MAINTAIN CONTROL. IF YOU DON'T ACCEPT THIS THEY WILL FIND OUT. THEY WILL SEND COPS TO SPY ON YOU, TO TAKE YOU AWAY. NO ONE CAN BE TRUSTED. SO I STAY VIGILANT. I WILL KILL IF I HAVE TO.

The court adjourned. The jury went home, under strict instruction to isolate themselves from any outside influences. How many of them obeyed, we will never know for sure. Surely all of them remembered something of the news coverage of the shooting, recycled on every news channel long before the trial began.

Ursula's words echoed in their minds as they ate dinner, as they lay in bed, unable to sleep.

Of course, it was all too easy for the jury to feel convinced of Ursula's guilt. A crazy old huntress with dead animals buried all around her home; a conspiracy theorist who lived alone, terrified of authority figures and possibly any kind of outsider. No great stretch of the imagination was needed to believe a woman like that – "deranged," wrote one local reporter[4] – was capable of murder, not only of a trooper, but also of a young woman. A poor,

---

4 Todd Greenblatt, "Trial begins for Fairbanks woman accused of two murders." *Anchorage Daily News*, February 13, 2017.

lost girl got mixed up with an evil old witch, a Big Bad Wolf in grandma's clothes, who only a brave woodcutter (Sweeney) managed to chop down.

It was a well-known story for the media to circulate and the prosecution to tap into, as good as truth. 'Insane' women, who disrupt the feminine ideals of serene wives, doting mothers and chaste daughters, perverting the model nuclear family, have, throughout our nation's history, been objects of fear and loathing. Certainly, Ursula is eccentric: for some, this is license enough to diagnose her with all the mental illnesses one wishes. And with the persistent stigma around mental illness, in media coverage leading up to and during the trial (a circus that undoubtedly influenced the jury's decision), Ursula was presented not as a vulnerable person in need of support and empathy, but as criminally insane. Besides "deranged," the epithet used most frequently in local reports to describe her was "hysterical."[5] How hysterical she sounded in her rambling statements. How hysterical she appeared in the courtroom: messy hair, yellow teeth, wild eyes. To the more 'sympathetic' commentators, Ursula had good reason to become hysterical: without a husband or children around to give her life structure and meaning, she must have felt empty, terrified, threatened. The isolation made her lose her mind. For without their appropriate place in society as wives and mothers, that's

---

5 Numerous instances of the word can be found in print and television news coverage of the murder trial; for example, see "Police killer Ursula Smith may have schizophrenia." *Fairbanks Daily News-Miner*, March 10, 2017.

supposedly what happens to women: they go crazy.

I was away on a work trip – myself unmarried, child-less – when I heard news of the verdict. Bored and alone in my hotel room, I caught one of the many TV documentaries broadcast hastily after Ursula's conviction, the type of documentary that cynically reconstructs a criminal case but offers no new insights. It was while watching this show – featuring the same old clip of Ursula being led into the courthouse; bird's eye views of her cabin and the evergreen swarms surrounding it; a shaky handheld camera panning a sequence of shots inside the cabin: the bloody table in the workroom, the gun rack, the sideboard decorated with photographs of a man and a boy – when a particular detail caught my attention. I couldn't believe I'd missed it before.

But why should I tell you about this case, you ask. First, let me tell you a little more about myself.

As a writer, I have always gone in search of interesting subjects. Like one of the intrepid explorers of old, during this search I cross murky waters, get lost in unchartered territories, blunder into dangerous bays. All too often the search is fruitless. Many times, I've had the desire to write but have not found the reason. When I was younger I tried to tackle fiction, before the lure of real-life mysteries and unresolved crimes inspired me to become an investigative journalist; a job that means being always on the lookout for a worthy subject. Sometimes you find the subject; sometimes the subject finds you.

Sitting in my hotel room, I realized the subject had found me. The detail I'd noticed couldn't be just a coincidence: it was more like the planets aligning. Jade, Ursula and I were three points spinning in the ether, light years apart from each other yet with orbits overlapping, converging.

At the time of writing, Jade has not been found, dead or alive. While the note and DNA found in Ursula's cabin indicate that Jade spent time there, to this day, no evidence has been found to prove that Jade was murdered. Meanwhile, Ursula sits in a jail cell, serving time for the first-degree murders of Sgt. Paul Mathers and of Jade Hunter.

If Ursula was wrongly convicted of Jade's murder, then Alaska's justice system failed both women. While the media branded Ursula as a madwoman in vivid and sensational detail, by comparison Jade slunk into obscurity. In all the reports I read and watched about Jade's disappearance and the police accusations of Ursula murdering her, I found scant information about Jade herself. Nothing beyond the fact she was a graduate student – her invitation to present her research at the academic conference hosted by UAF barely gets a mention – and brief descriptions of her physical appearance that focus on her being "young", "thin" and "petite". All of this gives Jade an impression of slightness, of being barely there; she takes up as little physical space as she occupies textual space in the news articles. Had the police and media been more curious about Jade, her interests, goals, desires – in short, had she been portrayed as anything more than an innocent victim who wandered blithely and naively into the woods – perhaps the investigation of her disappearance, as well as the outcome of Ursula's trial, might have taken a very different turn.

In 2017, following the guilty verdict, I embarked on a project that would hopefully shed light on the unfairness of the police investigations, media representation and legal proceedings that skewed this case. However, as more information about Jade became known – including, crucially, the document emailed to her PhD supervisor shortly before her disappearance – the nature of my project changed, taking me in directions I never could have imagined when I started. In the process I metamorphosed from an investigative journalist into something more akin to a mythmaker.

Before Jade's PhD supervisor finally came forward with the aforementioned document in January 2018, two questions nagged me during my research. First question: what makes a person jump on a plane and fly halfway around the globe to Alaska, abandon her legitimate reason for being there, i.e., the academic conference, and take off by herself into the wilderness?

Then again, stories not unlike this one are wearyingly familiar to Alaskans. Take the (in)famous story of Chris McCandless, the 24-year-old who left behind his comfortable life and affluent family in Virginian suburbia and embarked on a hitchhiking journey to Alaska, where he became a homeless poacher and was found dead in a vandalised Fairbanks bus in August 1992. Since then, McCandless has become a spiritual hero for many who, to this day, flock to Fairbanks from all over the continent each summer to experience their hero's journey for themselves. Though there is no evidence to suggest Jade was a McCandless fan or copycat (or that she had even heard of his story before arriving in Alaska), she seemed to fit the mould of young urban misfits from privileged backgrounds embarking on pilgrimages to Alaska, for whom the sparsely populated, largely uncultivated Last Frontier symbolises nature's sublime power and civilisation's vertiginous precipice.[6] Until Jade's document surfaced, this was my tentative answer to that first nagging question.

Second question: why has Jade never been found? Police found her DNA and handwritten note in Ursula's cabin, but they never found a body. If she didn't die there, where did

---

6 Alaskan writer Geoff Medraut complains of this in *Wildly Aspirational: The Cult of Chris McCandless* (Wolftooth Books, 2010): "While the Alaskan frontier remains a distant and near-mythological concept for many Americans, it is a mecca for explorers and nature lovers, as well as for a motley crew of middle class losers, weirdos, and no-hopers who believe their unique qualities and talents have been wasted within the confines of suburbia, college and white collar work. They allege that Alaska called to them, offering a new way of being" (p.15). According to Medraut, McCandless belonged firmly to the latter group as a college graduate turned poacher and thief; a bum who, after his death, somehow became a martyr for others of his ilk, inspiring Jon Krakauer's 1996 book, *Into the Wild*, and Sean Penn's 2007 film of the same name. At one point during his critique of McCandless's status as a cultural icon, Medraut displays a spectacularly dismissive attitude towards McCandless fans' sympathy and conjecture regarding their hero's mental state, in turn giving us a glimpse of our culture's endemic stigmatisation of mental illness: "Was he schizophrenic? Bipolar? Suffering narcissistic personality disorder? Probably. Tick all of the above. That might help explain his aversion to contributing to society" (p.32).

she go? What happened to her? Again, missing person cases are strangely familiar to Alaskans: many people have disappeared without a trace in the so-called Alaskan Bermuda Triangle.[7] Between 1990 and 2016, nine people from out-of-state went missing in the Fairbanks North Star Borough: six were eventually found dead in the wilderness and three, including Jade, have never been found.[8]

In most cases when an investigative journalist writes about a missing person or a murder case, the victim cannot speak: the journalist speaks for them, inventing their personalities, dreaming up motivations, assuming their desires. Part way through my project and my speaking for Jade, her thesis came to light, and suddenly she was telling her own story. As it turns out, my assumptions about Jade up to this point were far from accurate. It was my duty to let go of these and scrap what I'd written about her up to that point; otherwise, I'd be making the same mistakes as the media did leading up to Ursula's trial. For too long already, Jade had been spoken for, sidelined as a victim, footnoted in the case of her own disappearance. The only thing I could do was move aside and let her speak.

It was only by chance that I happened upon word of Jade's thesis. I was scrolling through Twitter when, serendipitously, I spotted a statement posted by Jade's PhD supervisor, who had shared a link to the document. By the

---

7 See Sheila B. Nickerson, *Disappearance, a Map: A Meditation on Death and Loss in the High Latitudes* (Doubleday, 1996).
8 See the Alaska Department of Public Safety's Missing Persons Clearinghouse, an online list of people who have been reported missing in Alaska.

time I clicked on it, however, the link no longer worked (shortly after, the supervisor deleted the post and, subsequently, his Twitter profile). Rumours spread that the document had already leaked online, but no one knew where. After scouring a shadowy, precarious corner of the web haunted by New Age spiritualists and occultists, I eventually located the document on a Neo-Arctolatry forum (for those not in the know, Neo-Arctolatry is the modern worship of bears).[9] Amazingly, beyond this forum and a few other marginal online communities, its emergence barely registered in the public eye. Presumably, police and Ursula's defence lawyers did not know what to do with the document, could not make head nor tail of it. The story was not picked up by the press. The world had moved on. The trial had already concluded, Ursula was jailed; other events now dominated the world stage in this most tumultuous period in our nation's history.

In Part One of this book, I present Jade's thesis. While certain editorial interventions have been made in the selection of this material and its presentation, very few changes have been made to the text itself. I have also judged several redactions necessary to avoid undue distress to her family, and some names and other identifying information have been changed.

In Part Two, I provide a reconstructed version of events

---

9 There are rumours that the thesis document is fake and at present this possibility cannot be entirely ruled out; however, a thorough fact-checking of certain details referred to within the text backs up my research into Jade's background, and so I firmly believe it is genuine.

from Ursula's perspective, informed by interviews with Ursula herself. It is not my intention to cause distress to the family of Paul Mathers or anyone else impacted by these tragedies. It is an attempt to probe deeper into a criminal case where justice has not been served. My hope for this book is twofold: first, I hope that it will motivate grassroots support for an appeal of the court's decision and eventual exoneration of Ursula for Jade's murder. Second, I hope that it will reignite search efforts for Jade, still missing after seven years.

Part One

Part One

ABSTRACT

In this thesis, part academic inquiry, part fairy tale and vision quest, I document a journey to Bear, whose teeth and claws will tear away the skin of this life, whose jaws are a gateway to the next. In embarking on this journey, I test a hypothesis informed by etymological, literary and socio-cultural readings of the bear.

My predictions for this experiment are as follows: it will happen as it always happens in the stories: a girl wanders deep into the forest where hunger lurks. She strays from the path. The beast smells her blood, hears her racing heart, embraces her like a lover. It is the kind of love colloquially understood to 'make you want to eat [someone] up'. Being fed upon feels like more love than she thought possible. In the belly of the beast, she waits to be reborn.

Both predator and prey are transformed in this transaction of life and death, in the exchange of energies enacted by the digestive process. Being prey in the food chain is alien to most humans, a fate generally found only in fairy tales, and never personally experienced by the vast majority in real life; on rare occasions when animals do feed on humans, they are perceived as anomalies, freak accidents. Yet despite (or because of) their fear of preydom, humans are drawn to the idea of feeding; for millennia, it has inspired iconography (such as the ouroboros, the serpent eating its own tail), language, religious ritual, oral tradition and literature.

I perform another retelling of the fairy tales fed to us and ruminated on, over and over, for generations – in retelling those stories we hear the voices of ghosts, the whispers of ages long gone. I hear my mother, who, in her dying moments, gaped and bared her teeth: as though, as the life left her body in this realm, she prepared to swallow another.

Eat me, drink me: I am falling down the rabbit hole, down the world's gullet. This is the last supper and I am the bread and wine. Bear will lick me into shape.

INTRODUCTION: HIBERNATION ENDS

i.   *THE GREEN MAN*

The garden grows no grass, no flowers, only weeds that punch angry, green fists through the flagstones. It's more like a tip than a garden. All manner of detritus somehow finds its way there, just as we, the tenants, have ended up in Otto's house. From the mountain of rubbish piled high in the centre we drag out legs from broken chairs, bits of fencing, wooden crates splintered out of shape. Anything that will burn.

Otto picks up his hand axe, bends over the crates and fence posts and chops them into small logs. When he's finished, he stands tall, rolls his broad shoulders back and flicks his sweat-soaked hair out of his face. A droplet of sweat lands on my lip, cool and salty. He doesn't say it, but I can tell he is enjoying himself; that he takes pride in physical labour and working with his hands. He can almost pretend that we are living in a real commune, camping deep in the countryside, not boxed in a three-storey Victorian house in Chorlton that Otto bought with the fortune he'd made from designing software a decade ago. In his previous life.

The rest of us stand around, waiting for instruction. Anaïs shivers in her parka and blows on her hands, while Rory, pale and lugubrious, dressed in a military jacket and his favourite The Smiths *Meat is Murder* t-shirt, distracts himself from his hangover nausea with his phone.

Otto drops the axe and wipes his hands on his legs, smearing gritty black marks on the khaki fabric of his combat trousers. The stains suit his look. He makes a considered effort to dress without care or attention, purposefully selecting clothes in drab colours, bargain rack finds. He avoids designer labels, of course. His anti-fashion is a fashion choice, complementing his effortless good looks. Sometimes when we watch TV together in the living room and I'm flicking through the channels, he'll scoff at the current trend of programmes concerned with fashion, at the vanity and desperation of all the people who give it credence. I mentioned once that my mum had loved clothes; that when I was thirteen, my dad splashed out on a gift for their wedding anniversary: an antique coat made from real mink fur.

"What did you say to her?" Otto had asked.

"I didn't say anything. I snuck into her wardrobe and threw red paint all over it."

"Good girl."

I bristled when he said that; the same way I bristled when Mum first showed me her coat. Something had died in me, trying to be Otto's Good Girl, like how something had died to produce Mum's coat. I remember running my fingers through the soft black fur; and later, hearing Mum shout my full name, the fury and mourning in her voice when she discovered what I'd done. I was angry with her too. We had been angry at each other for so long, for so much of the time. Sometimes it's hard to remember the good times. Chatting to her on the phone. Her laughter. Her hand on my cheek.

With the exception of Otto, we all feel better when we're back inside, stoking the fire, stuffing balls of newspaper on top of the logs we'd just collected and piled into the stove. The fire glows before bursting into life, popping and cracking merrily. We sit before it in a circle. Warmth spreads into our icy fingers. I begin to relax, until Otto wraps his arm around my waist. Anaïs chatters in her soft French lilt, drawing us all in with that gentle way she has; even Rory's hangover is wearing off. She asks us what we'd prefer for dinner: falafel or pasta? I feel Otto fidgeting beside me, growing restless. He sits up straight, clears his throat, takes charge of the conversation.

"We should plan our next protest," he says.

An awkward silence descends. Rory keeps his eyes down on his hands in his lap. Anaïs looks uncomfortable, hesitating to speak.

"What about the injunction?" she asks, finally.

"What about it?" Otto scoffs.

Anaïs looks at Otto gravely. "We could go to prison."

"Prison's nothing compared to extinction."

"Bastards," Rory mutters, without elaboration. There's no need. We all know who the bastards are, taking out injunctions after our last protest to protect their drilling sites. I'd wanted to bring them down too, until... until. I attempt to shuffle out from under Otto's arm. Anaïs watches me: she knows something's off between Otto and me, that the equilibrium in the house has shifted.

"Still," sighs Rory, "I mean, *prison*..."

"We can't let them scare us off that easily. Not while they're continuing to destroy the world and profit from it," Otto declares. He tightens his arm around my waist. "Jade's with me on this."

I say nothing. Otto casts me a sidelong glance.

"You're in, aren't you, Jade?"

How can I explain to him? Things have changed.

I am transforming.

ii.   *THE MINOTAUR*

I was lost.[10]

The Faculty of Arts building was labyrinthine, its corridors winding and dividing unexpectedly into more corridors. I focused on the signs mounted on the wall beside each room: SW LG 1.23, SW LG 1.24, WW LG 1.01. The South Wing gave way to the West Wing which in turn gave way, unfathomably, to the East Wing; for some reason the North Wing could not be found. Though I'd attended lectures and seminars here for almost five years, I consistently lost all sense of direction the moment I stepped into the foyer, squared up by the Doric columns that reached up to the basilica-like domed ceiling, by the marble busts of dead intellectuals who glared stonily at me: just another student with naive ideas and vague opinions. Now that I was a research student, I only had to visit my supervisor's office, located somewhere on the Lower Ground floor, for an occasional meeting. But my memory of how to get there eluded me.

By the time I found my supervisor's office I was sweating. The office door was closed. My supervisor's name was embossed on a placard mounted in the centre – DR STEPHEN BELL – above a laminated sign printed with his office hours: Mondays 3-5pm. I held my hand out, knuckles poised to knock, before drawing it back. I was five minutes

---

10   Editor's note: Jade's sudden switch to past tense in this section suggests that the episode recounted here took place before the episode recounted in Introduction, i. THE GREEN MAN.

early. Judging from the two previous supervisions I'd had with Dr Bell, he didn't seem like the kind of man who would appreciate being disturbed. Following the submission of my research proposal, a faculty committee matched us up; Dr Bell had authored a book about North American folklore in the 90s. Despite our overlapping research interests, we had little else in common; our conversations have been awkward and stilted. He'd cut our last two meetings short. I sensed I was an inconvenience, an irritating distraction from more important work he wanted to do.

I leaned back against the opposite wall and read and re-read the posters pinned to the notice board: an essay competition, the Middle English Poetry Society meeting on Tuesdays, the University's state-of-the-art research facilities. Somewhere down the long, narrow corridor came the echoes of distant conversations; from the floor above, the thudding pulse of footsteps approaching and disappearing. I listened out for the sound of voices in Dr Bell's office but couldn't tell if there were or weren't any.

My jumper prickled and itched against my skin. I pulled it off. I checked my phone: a text from Otto. *Where are you? When will you be home?* I hadn't told him about my supervision meeting; I hadn't had one in months, hadn't opened my laptop and done any solid work until a few weeks ago. He wouldn't like that I'd turned my attention back to something else. Otto never asked about my work. Whenever I tried to explain my research, he would fidget, eyes glazed over, tracking with an impatient "Yeah" or "Mmm" or "Right" until he could change the subject to something he knew more about than I did. Once, after we'd met a Creative Writing PhD student at a march, Otto muttered later about how arrogant, how self-indulgent they were: "Why the fuck would you need a PhD to be a poet?" I'd laughed along although I was secretly hurt, sensing that the jab had really been meant for me. Why was I doing a PhD, I wondered. What was the point of it? Yet here I was. I wasn't done. Something about the work had been niggling me, calling to me for weeks. Like a puzzle I was on the edge of solving.

A trickle of sweat ran down my spine; my chest had erupted with dark red blotches. I scrabbled to pull my jumper back on, leaned against the wall and took deep breaths. Focusing on my breathing only made me aware of the tightness of my lungs. I fixed my gaze on the worn carpet, its curling synthetic fibres, blue and brash and ugly. I tried to imagine that instead I stood on deep snow, where cold radiated from my feet up my legs and into my heart.

The door swung open. Dr Bell stuck out his head: small, balding, spectacled. His eyes narrowed. I wondered if he remembered who I was; he never addressed me by my name in person, only in email, which had led me to question whether he had ever put my name and my face together in his mind.

"I thought I heard someone out there," he said. Dr Bell was Canadian, probably in his late fifties or early sixties. He reminded me of my dad, who also always wore the same expression – a thin smile – regardless of whether he was pleased or annoyed. He spoke slowly, selecting his words exactly, before upending his sentences with a little whine of impatience. "Come in, come in," he sighed.

Dr Bell gestured towards a seat opposite his desk. His office was small and cramped with bookshelves. I spotted several copies of his own books, recognising the titles of his novels and volumes of literary criticism (these texts had been assigned to my undergraduate reading list). He tutted a vague tune as he clicked on and read something on his computer screen. I wondered if he was waiting for me to speak first. Or had forgotten I was there.

"So, I read the draft of your chapter," he said, finally. I was sitting up very straight, perched on the end of my seat.

"I read it and, I have to say, I'm a little confused." He smiled. Was it an ironic smile? Was there pity in it? Amusement? I felt my cheeks glow.

"Oh?" was all I could muster in response.

He licked his lips. His chair squeaked as he leaned back and neatly folded his hands across his stomach. "It's not academic research," he said, simply.

I waited for him to explain but instead he looked at me, expectantly. He liked to do something similar in his lectures: pick on a student, pronounce a bold statement or pose a direct question, then wait for a response. Everyone else in the room would stare while the student fumbled for the answer Dr Bell wanted to hear. He reserved his most withering look for a student who fed back the 'wrong' answer. As an undergraduate I was always afraid of going to his lectures, but he never picked on me, never noticed I was there.

"I don't understand," I said, truthfully.

31

"It's not academic research," he repeated, cocking his head, surveying me over his glasses. "It's – well – I'm not sure what to call it."

"I know I need to look at the theory a bit more," I tried to explain. "I know there are some claims in there that aren't substantiated properly. I've not done my references yet –"

He held a hand up for me to stop. "I just have one question. Why bears?"

The question struck me like a slap.

"Well, why not bears?" I spluttered back, cringing at the petulant tone of my voice. But Dr Bell didn't even seem to register it.

"Your topic is a very broad subject – human-animal transformations in fairy tales and folklore – but you've focused almost exclusively on humans transforming into bears and vice versa. You don't provide any particular reasoning for this or anything to situate your area of concern in recent academic debate. Your argument is unclear and doesn't provide a critical engagement with the texts. Frankly, the whole chapter is rather... erratic. And all this reference to some recent bear attacks in the news – ah, I'm afraid I don't see what relevance this has to literary analysis."

I didn't know how to respond. Even if I had known, I could barely speak. My tongue felt swollen and stupid in my mouth.

He leaned forward in his chair, clicked and scrolled through something on his computer. In his dingy little office, surrounded by books, he looked every inch the professor. His wool suit fit him like a second skin, or perhaps a first skin – he was the thing he was supposed to be and had never considered an existence beyond it. He was perfectly self-contented. I envied him. He clicked again before returning his attention to me.

"What I would suggest is going back to the drawing board. Ask yourself again what it is that you are researching. What's your thesis?"

What was my thesis? The question was huge and monstrous. He might as well have asked: what is your purpose in life? I looked down at my hands clutching the seat. He was waiting for me to answer, amused and vindicated and disappointed that, of course, I couldn't. Or perhaps he wasn't at all. Perhaps he was just being friendly and offering good advice, had just asked a rhetorical question, posed an invitation to think. Or maybe he didn't care either way, would forget about me as soon as I left his office.

Something strange was happening to my hands. My fingers were fusing together. The dips between my knuckles were growing shallower. Veins ridging the backs of my hands smoothed out. It was a curious sensation; I observed it like an outsider. My tongue melted into the roof of my mouth; I felt my nose and lips sink into my face, submerged in sheets of skin, while tiny white lights popped in the corners of my eyes and a scream rang in my ears; I was losing my sight, losing my hearing, losing all form and shape, growing into a pink, amorphous thing...

"Come back in a month or so when you've got another

draft," drawled Dr Bell, oblivious to my metamorphosis.[11]

11 Editor's note: Dr Bell no longer teaches at Jade's alma mater and seemingly has not continued his academic career elsewhere; I have been unable to track down his details at any other institution. Shortly after he shared Jade's thesis online and posted a Twitter statement – to the effect that he felt he had withheld the document for too long, that he could no longer bear it, although the exact wording is lost – within hours the statement was deleted, and within days his Twitter profile and author website shut down. He didn't show up to any classes after that. His friends and colleagues said he left town but they haven't heard from him since. His teaching contract was finally terminated in April 2018. He provided no forwarding address after his faculty email address became defunct. Until any new information about the erstwhile teacher and author emerges, for all we know, Dr Bell has vanished from the face of the earth.

iii   *ECHO AND NARCISSUS*

"Is something wrong?" Otto asks.

I mumble that it's nothing, slip into bed, shuffle to the outermost edge. Hoping he'll get the message. But he climbs in and spoons me, his arm stealing across my side, his beard scouring my neck. His breath is hot and close, milky and sweet, smelling unmistakably of Otto, its mingled affection and arousal cloying.

His mouth hovers directly over my ear, whispering too close, too loud: "I bet I can make you feel better."

I'm another problem he presumes to fix if only he could be given a chance. All the world's problems are within his ability to fix, and if only he had the authority – but, tragically, he's never had the authority.

He plants a kiss on my shoulder. And another. Hard, heavy bumps of the mouth, clumsy like a child's.

"I love you."

His fingertips trace the curve of my belly; how can something so gentle feel like a vice?

"I love you, Jade."

The tone in his voice is now questioning, expectant: he awaits my echo. He says 'I love you' only to hear the words back.

All I have to say is: no. I don't want this.

But I don't.

I don't have a clear argument.

Especially when you look at the facts: Otto is a good man – surely that is how anyone would describe him. He's generous. He cares about the world. He's a person of conviction. And, for some reason, he loves me. He is good to me, letting me live here, rent-free; through Otto I have not only a home, but a bigger purpose: I have protests, petitions, marches.

How to describe myself? Shapeless. A lacuna. An echo.

In his arms I am a lump of meat. Out of his arms I am a lump of meat.

My muscles behave as they are wont to behave, flinching as he pulls down my underwear, as he moves himself into the lump of meat that is my body: merely a sequence of stimuli and response, a code of flesh and bone, pre-programmed and predictable in its sensations and motions; a mass that yields.

So, I remove thoughts from this body and take them away, far away, to a place where I'll never be found, where I'm swallowed up.

And it comes to me suddenly: that magic, missing ingredient.

It's still there afterwards, in the dark chill of an unhappy bedroom: an idea that grows, undeterred by the frenetic rise and fall of Otto's naked chest, by heaving breath and the rustle of bedsheets, clammy against my legs. Our bodies untangle, cold and separate once again, desires secretly, perpetually disappointed. We are moths bumping into each other under artificial light, drawn to the glow of something we cannot touch.

But Otto cannot bear solitude. He reaches over again, this time just to hold me; he has romanticised the idea of us falling asleep in each other's arms. I pull away – I can't sleep otherwise – turning my back to him and perching on the edge of the bed. Mercifully, he gives up and turns away. But now, I decide, I will not sleep. Alone, uninterrupted, I can think. I listen for what might be minutes or hours as Otto's breathing steadies and softens – meanwhile, the pulse in my temple thuds faster, faster.

I am forming a plan.

CHAPTER ONE
Circles and Tongues

i. *SUMMER IS BEAR SEASON*

June 27th   Black bear attack in Pogo Mine (East of
                 Fairbanks, Alaska)*

July 10th   Black bear attack at Lake George / Delta
                 Junction (Southeast of Fairbanks)*

July 16th   Grizzly bear attack in Denali National Park
                 (Southwest of Fairbanks)

August 4th   Black bear attack at Two Rivers (East of
                 Fairbanks)

August 7th   Black bear attack in Chatanika (Northeast
                 of Fairbanks)*

* Fatal

'Sixth fatal bear attack in two years in Interior Alaska raises alarm'

The killing of a hiker by a black bear on July 10, 2015, the sixth
fatal bear attack to occur in two years in Alaska's Interior region,
has raised concerns among local authorities.

Don Lymond, 35, was hiking near Delta Junction on July 10 when a bear attacked and killed him. Hours after Lymond was reported missing, his remains were found by police dogs and an autopsy confirmed that he had died from a bear attack. On July 12, wildlife biologists shot and killed an adult male black bear found in the vicinity, and a necropsy revealed that the bear had human remains in its stomach.

"This tragic incident is unfortunately the latest in a series of bear attacks in the area," said Pete Ford, Department of Fish and Game spokesman, in a statement following Lymond's death.

"It is not known if it was a predatory attack or whether it started out as defensive and became a predatory attack. It's very rare for bears to exhibit predatory behaviour, but what we've witnessed is a dramatic increase in these kinds of unprovoked, aggressive behaviours in recent years. That's very concerning indeed."

Fish and Game also point to a sharp rise in the number of bear sightings in the region since 2013.

"The frequency of these kinds of conflicts between bears and humans is totally unprecedented. Bears tend to avoid humans, but a lot of experts are saying that as the human population grows, bears are coming into contact with humans more often, they're hearing noises made by people more, so they're becoming less afraid."

In July last year, people in Fairbanks, Alaska were warned to stay away from the Chena River hiking trails and forest areas after three people were killed in a spate of bear attacks. The attacks were believed to have been committed by one bear that, according to local vet Paige Sullivan, "may have realised it could eat humans after tasting human flesh for the first time."

In the wake of last year's attacks, conservation officers killed ten bears suspected of being involved in the killings, but DNA tests were not able to confirm if any of the bears had been involved. The killings sparked an outcry among local animal rights and environmental groups, including Green Frontier, who argued that the bear killings were unnecessary and disorganised, and that more work should be done to prevent people from encroaching on bear habitats, in an interview with the Anchorage Daily News last year.

On July 12, 2015, Green Frontier posted a statement on their Facebook page, stating that "[while] Don Lymond's death was a tragedy, we should all be appalled and concerned about the draconic and ill-thought-out counteractive measures used by the Dept. of Fish and Game, including a MASS BEAR CULL. Once again assuming human superiority over the rest of the world."

The post was deleted from the site later that day.

Ford made no comment on rumours that local authorities are considering a mass bear cull in the area as a measure to counteract the attacks, but warned people to be vigilant:

"Stay away from areas where bears have been sighted. It's very rare for bears to attack humans and so it's difficult to predict this kind of behaviour, but for now we are asking people to exercise caution."[12]

---

12 Editor's note: In this section of the thesis, Jade commits academic treason: she provides no sources. I have been unable to locate the original source of this article, although several local and state-wide news websites ran reports on this bear attack in 2015.

The Woman Who Loved a Bear

Long ago there lived a woman with many suitors but she refused to marry, even though her father chided and her brothers teased. Her mother was not there to weigh in on the matter; she had died giving birth to the youngest boy. The woman went out to get wood each day and returned to the camp later and later as time went on. Her brothers grew suspicious and then one day they followed her into the brush, going quietly, spying between the trees. There they discovered their sister's secret: she had taken a bear as a lover.

The Woman Who Married a Bear

At the outer limits of the world, amidst the forests and snow-topped mountains, lived a young woman with her family. The woman was proud and ignored her family's pleas to respect the bears who ruled the forests. One day, while she was out gathering berries, the woman stepped in bear dung and cursed aloud. The bears overheard her and decided they would make her pay the price. The woman became drowsy as the afternoon grew warm and she lay down by the river. Within minutes she fell asleep. When she awoke, before her stood the most handsome man she had ever seen, and she loved him at once. He beckoned, and she followed him through the mountain pass to his village. But when she arrived at his lodge, the biggest in the village, and he took off his tunic, he was no longer a man, but a bear. 'You are my wife now,' he said. At first she was angry. But as the seasons passed she fell in love again and bore his children. Then the woman's brothers discovered that their sister had been forced to marry the Bear Chief and swore vengeance when they found her. When her brothers came, her husband would not attack them, letting them kill him instead. With his last words, he addressed his wife, asking her to return to her people and teach them to respect the bears.[13]

13 Editor's note: I was also unable to locate the original source of these folktale excerpts. Very similar versions of both stories appear on numerous websites, where Jade may have appropriated the details. The stories are based on the oral traditions of indigenous cultures in Western Canada and the northwest coast of North America, including the Tlingit and Athabascan peoples. See Catharine McLellan, "The Girl Who Married the Bear: a masterpiece in Indian oral tradition." *Publications in Ethnology, 2.* (Ottawa: National Museums of Canada, 1970).

CHAPTER TWO

Callisto

Conference Call for papers

The 4th Global Symposium on Fairy Tales, Fables and Folklore (FFF) is the premier forum for the presentation of new academic research, creative writing and performance art related to the study of folk literature. This prestigious event provides an international platform for academics, students, writers, artists and other creative practitioners to present their work. A peripatetic event, the Symposium has previously been held in Copenhagen, Denmark (2010), Marburg, Germany (2012), and Paris, France (2014). We are thrilled to announce that FFF will be travelling across the Atlantic to our friends in the United States of America for our next event on 11-15 April 2016, hosted by University of Alaska Fairbanks.

We are seeking proposals for sessions organised around a theme, special panels, and/or individual papers/performances. Sessions are scheduled in ninety-minute slots, typically with three twenty-minute presentations plus a thirty-minute Q&A per standard session. As always, proposals on any topic related to fairy tales, fables, folklore/oral tradition are warmly welcomed.

Please submit abstracts/proposals by 1 December 2015 to be considered for our 2016 symposium.

i.

"Why are you doing this?"

Otto stands over me, slightly stooped forward (he hunches his shoulders like other insecure tall people), eyebrows raised, forehead creased up. I look past his incredulity and focus on the lines on his face, thinking of trees and how you can count the rings of bark to guess their age. Otto's wrinkles betray him in the same way as his height; he is insecure about both; approaching forty, living with a group of twenty-something-year-olds who any day might up and leave him, overgrown and awkward and stumbling through a world of subtle details he can't grasp.

"What's so funny?"

"Nothing."

"This isn't funny. Going on a big holiday like this without even consulting me."

"It's not a holiday. It's a conference. And it's not a definite yet – I've only submitted an abstract. They have to accept me first." I hesitate, swallow; my throat is getting dry. Fuck it.

"And I don't need to consult you," I add.

His face changes: now it is a storm cloud.

"Apparently not. But maybe you should have. I mean, going all that way for a conference for five days. Is it really

47

worth the money? Or the carbon footprint? This is such a part of the problem, why the atmosphere's a mess, when people take long haul flights without considering the consequences."

"Maybe I'm planning on staying there a bit longer than five days."

"Oh, really? Longer?" he balks. Then he changes tack, sneering: "I take it Daddy's paying for this?"

I flare up with anger as I recognise the cheap shot. He wields my family's wealth like a weapon against me; the material privilege I'd been brought up with as a child, thanks to my dad's job at an oil company, made all my adult decisions questionable. Under scrutiny, his logic would surely seem better than my logic.

I breathe calmly; I'd thought this all out in advance. I reply coolly: "Of course my dad isn't paying. I wouldn't ask him to. My scholarship includes funding for conference attendance. They're actually really keen for PhD candidates to represent the institution internationally at these types of events. I expect they'll probably cover the airfare and accommodation, plus the attendance fee."

Otto sighs deeply, making a real show of shaking his head, at his wit's end.

"So, when is it then? April, right?"

This is the tricky part, though obviously I'm not going to explain any of this to Otto; from my research I realise it would have been better to go in the summer, ideally July. But this was the only chance I had. There were other ways to travel to Alaska, of course – package adventure holidays in its national parks, companies offering guided tours of glaciers and lakes, nature trails, some even promising bear sightings – but none that I could afford. Nor did they offer the type of journey I was planning; I would be going much further than a carefully supervised holiday for tourists would allow. Better to have more control over the trip, and to control the story I would tell people about the trip I would be taking.

If I had the money, I would have just booked a one-way plane ticket, and there would be no need to apply to attend the conference. But even that would have cost nearly a grand. As Otto well knows, I don't ask my dad for money anymore, though he could have afforded a grand easily. I'd turned to Dad for a loan in the past: during my undergrad studies when I lost my part-time job, then halfway through my master's degree when my last boyfriend broke up with me and chucked me out of his flat. I'd felt regretful and seedy when the deposit appeared in my account: oil money, and I was benefiting from it. Eventually I acknowledged the hypocrisy. I stopped asking for more, which made things simpler; Dad's money always came with strings attached. Knowing I'd never be able to pay him back, he'd expect something else in return: taking a job at his company; something in marketing, perhaps. Certainly, giving up this "Greenpeace nonsense". Or leaving Otto.

At this point, even if I did ask Dad for money, he'd probably refuse. He'd given up hope. Ever since I'd delivered the news that I had no intention of pursuing any of the lucrative careers he'd suggested for me, and that I was still with Otto and remained an activist, he'd written me off, financially speaking. Better to let the university and the AHRC fund my trip. Technically, it is for "research".

Otto might have lent me the money, or even paid for the whole trip – I am sure of this, despite the protestations about environmental impact he had just made – but only on the condition he would come too. But he'll interfere with my plan, I know he will. He's held me back for too long already.

I have to go alone.

I see in his face now something of a terrified child who knows for certain that the monster is real; that this is happening, really happening. All his fear of abandonment brims in his eyes. In the past, when I placed so little value on my own life, I would have rushed to make his easier. "I'm sorry. I'm being selfish. It's alright, I won't go. They probably wouldn't have accepted my paper anyway," I'd have said.

But I've shed my old self like dead skin.

Otto is irrelevant. I don't care if I'm selfish. I'm going.

I'll make sure of that.

ii.

I'm jittery, full of adrenalin. I've left Otto downstairs looking seriously pissed off. He's not used to not getting his own way. But it's late and freezing outside, and there's nowhere else to go but back up to his room.

Nothing to do but wait.

I pace around the room. A few months ago, I saw a documentary about animals in captivity. It showed clip after clip of caged lions, tigers, chimpanzees. There was one clip of a bear lurching from one side of its cage to another, again and again, locked in a frantic loop. I had that image stuck in my head for days afterwards. It made me think of all the pets I'd had as a child. A goldfish in a tank. A hamster that used to run circles in a plastic wheel, or inside a ball whenever I felt like scooping it out of its steel-barred box. We briefly owned a dog that no one walked enough, so it barked all day in the garden, whining when it jumped up and pawed at the fence, until Dad decided it was a nuisance and had to go. It was probably put down. All those creatures, swallowed alive by walls and metal bars, doomed to live out their natural lives in traps. I felt their desperation, the hurt of life clamped down and stolen.

Maybe it was just to exorcise the image of the caged bear replaying in my head, but I ended up searching YouTube for videos of bears in the wild. The first video I found was of black bears catching salmon in Alaska. The camera panned over them standing firm in a gushing river, holding their balance despite the strong current, their glossy coats slick and wet. One of them snapped up a wriggling salmon at just the right moment. The salmon stood no chance; it gawped and gave itself up to those powerful jaws. It was the most beautiful video I'd ever seen.

Now I crawl into Otto's bed, shivering with nervous, unspent energy and from this drizzly Mancunian winter that drains my vitality – not like the brutal intensity of

Alaskan winters, where life is pushed to extremes and survival is a miracle. I am done with hibernating, done with sleepwalking through life. Yet somehow I must bide my time here until spring.

The yellowed bedsheets smell of stale sweat and semen. Of all those times I didn't know how to say no to him. There'd only been two others before Otto. A boy whose face I don't remember; I was drunk at a Freshers' party. The one after – Oscar – I latched onto during my master's. He lost interest in me after I told him my mum was dying. I was too immature for him, he said, the responsibility was too much. It was probably something to do with Mum's illness, but after Oscar broke up with me, I had an urge to take more chances. I applied for the PhD programme and scholarship.

A year later, I met Otto.

Even before I met Otto himself, his house was exactly what I'd been looking for. *£150pcm room in all-vegan eco-house share*, the listing on Gumtree had read. *Seeking a like-minded 3rd housemate to come and join our friendly family!!* The cheapness appealed; cheap accommodation on top of a funded PhD meant there was no excuse to ask Dad for money again. More than that, I wanted a complete restart. Mum had died a month before; I no longer had to live with her illness, which had come to define me, suffusing everything I did with the anticipation of her death. When it finally happened, I felt empty, numb. Otto had been prepared to share everything: his house, his bed, his life's purpose. That purpose was much greater than me. It had been easy to move into Otto's home and then easy to give in to

Otto entirely. Both had swallowed me whole.

The duvet has coiled itself tight around my legs. Gritty sheets scratch my bare, frozen toes. I kick to free myself.

Never will I let anyone lock me in again.

iii.

He slides into bed behind me, wrapping his hands around my stomach. So, he's decided to forgive me. Or he believes he'll find a way to change my mind, all in good time.

"I didn't mean to upset you," he whispers, kissing my neck. "I still don't think you should go, but it's up to you."

I flinch from his creeping hands and lips, those maggot swarms, feeding on me like I'm already a corpse. When I speak my voice is low and hoarse, barely human.

"Don't touch me."

I can only make out his silhouette in the dark, lying frozen on his side, but I can tell he is shocked.

"What the fuck is wrong with you?"

He fakes a laugh, mocking my rejection of him as though I'm having another of my petty outbursts. Laughter at others having the wrong opinions or the wrong reactions is his default response. Only the childish, escalating pitch of his voice betrays him.

I'm on my side, facing away from him, perched on the edge of the bed. My shoulders are rigid. He huffs, impatiently waiting for me to apologise. I do nothing of the sort. I do nothing at all – I lie there, made of stone; a monolith indifferent to his needs. Funny: we have lain beside one another doing nothing so many times before during our road-blocks, when we held hands and lay down together on the tarmac, unflinching at the honks of car horns and shouting crowds and approaching footsteps of police. "Usually doing nothing is easy," he'd tell us in his pep talk before the protest. "Most people do nothing and let the world burn. But a peaceful protest is the hardest thing. That kind of doing nothing is an art form. The difference is it's not for yourself – it's for the greater good."

His hand is on my shoulder, warm and clammy. He shakes me gently at first, then more insistently.

"What's wrong?" he whispers. His tone has changed, all mockery evaporated. "Did I –? Are you okay?"

He's only going to keep pestering. I might as well come clean. "Something happened to me."

His hand softens and the tension leaves his voice: he's relieved to get an answer out of me, finally, and to be proven correct. "Thought so. You've been acting so weird. What happened?"

"I've changed."

"Changed what?"

"Otto," I sigh and turn to face him. I choose my words carefully; I don't want to tell him everything. "I'm not the person you knew."

"What're you on about?"

"It's not going to be the same between us anymore."

"What are you saying, exactly?"

I hear the creaking bone of his jaw working. "Is there

someone else?" His voice is much lower now, barely perceptible.

"I can understand if you want me out of the house. I'll
be gone soon anyway."

He jolts onto his knees and leans over me, his angular
silhouette charged with a dark energy fuelled by confusion
and rage.

"What do you mean, you'll be 'gone soon'?"

He flicks the bedside lamp on. The shadows on his face
are thrown into relief by bright yellow light. It hurts my
eyes.

"I mean I'll be going to the conference," I say quickly. "If
they accept my paper."

"I am so fucking sick of hearing about this conference."

He flings the covers off his legs and lurches out of bed,
seizes a pair of jeans and a crumpled t-shirt from the mess
on the carpet.

"It's funny," he says as he tugs on his jeans, "how all of
a sudden, you're obsessed with that. You weren't exactly a
dedicated student before. Honestly, I thought you'd have
packed in your degree by now, since it's clearly going
nowhere." He pulls the t-shirt over his head, flicks his hair
out from under the collar. "Not that I'd mind if you did.
The world hardly needs another arts PhD. Reading fairy
tales isn't exactly researching how to reverse global warm-
ing, is it?" He pulls a hoodie off a pile of clothes strewn on
his desk chair. "But that didn't bother me because I thought
you cared about more important things. Apparently not."

He slams the door on his way out of the room. I turn

out the lamp, relieved for the quiet and darkness, and turn over, trying to ignore the sharp, persistent pain in my chest.

iv.

The other side of the bed is still empty when I wake up. Late morning light creeps around the edges of the blind, painting the walls a sombre grey. Otto's pop art print of Che Guevara, normally bright with lime and forest hues – an ode to environmentalism and socialism combined – is muted and monochrome. In this light, the mess in the room looks like the aftermath of a bomb. Only that's how it has always looked; I'd just grown used to it and stopped seeing the chaos.

I pad to the en suite bathroom. Peering into the mirror, I inspect the changes. This is what the others must see. Jade's ghost – her simulacrum. She moves with me, copies Jade's appearance, speaks in her voice, approximates her habits and gestures. Only I seem able or care to look beneath the phantom layer.

Where my old face had definition, now the hollows run smooth: nostrils sealed over, eyes coated in some kind of membrane, gossamer thin. My mouth is a long slit; the lips are gone. My new skin is soft, raw and pink, like a newborn's. Unmarked, featureless. No freckles or moles. I hold up my hands: barely recognisable as hands, their intricate, dextrous bone structure lost, the lines on the palms and knuckles gone. The only feature of Jade's that remains is the

56

tattoo on my wrist of a serpent swallowing its own tail. I look closer at my new mouth. It opens wider than a mouth should. I open as wide as I can and have a crater in my head.

I sink onto the tiles, noting their familiar cracks, their coating of dust, pubic hairs, toenail clippings and dead skin. I lie back on the cold, hard floor and shut my eyes. I'm no longer in a bathroom: I'm lying on a frozen lake. I inhale the fresh mountain air and pine from the nearby forest. The ice creaks under the immense weight of the body now approaching with fur redolent of earth and undergrowth and its own particular animal stink. Its muzzle brushes my face. Hot breath blows across my cheeks and saliva drops like rain; I taste the juice of blackberries just eaten. Tips of teeth rake the edges of my mouth: we could be kissing. All it would have to do is snap its mighty jaws and it would end me, begin me again.

The tiles are back beneath me: I feel their cracks. Alaska feels so close and out of reach all at once.

v.

I sit in bed and work on my thesis through the afternoon until my back aches. When I stand up to relieve it, my spine creaks; the sound is like ice cracking. The change goes deeper than skin level, then. My bones are breaking up, nerves splitting and disintegrating.

I wander through the house, not my home for much longer, I hope – my time spent here already feels like the past, has that feeling of things dead and gone, like I'm walking through a museum of my own memories. On the top floor, Otto's room and en suite, which I have shared, along with his opinions and desires, for nearly a year. Down the first staircase are Anaïs's and Rory's rooms and the communal bathroom, which Anaïs takes upon herself to clean meticulously once a week. On the landing, she has hung a wreath from the loose nail crookedly sticking out of the wall and laced red and green tinsel around the banister leading down to the hallway.

Downstairs, the door to the front room – or the parlour, as its Victorian inhabitants would have called it – is closed, as always. On my first night here, when I'd agreed to rent the room Anaïs is in now ("no contracts here," Otto had informed me, "I'm not the devil, I don't make you sign your soul away"), he threw a little welcome party. He invited friends over and encouraged Rory and me to do the same. He had actually tidied up the place, laid a spread of snacks and beer for us to share. Part way through the evening there was a power cut. After all the lights went off, Otto disappeared and came back with his arms full of candles and tealights. He placed them around the parlour on every bit of spare space: on windowsills, bookshelves, on top of the broken grand piano. We were like kids whose parents had gone away and left us to our own devices: we stayed up all night in the candlelit room, singing and plunking the piano keys, which thrummed with strange off-key vibrations. We chatted and laughed and shared spliffs, the lit ends glowing orange in the dark.

Otto told anecdotes about his time living in an eco-village in Spain – how he came back to the UK determined to create a similar setup in Manchester, a place where like-minded people lived together with a common purpose. Chosen family, he called it. The old house with its dusty, eclectic furniture, its shambolic nooks and crannies, felt like a family member itself: the grandfather, perhaps, full of quirks and eccentricities.

I would start a whole new life here, I decided then; turn my back on years of disastrous student accommodation and renting overpriced hovels – and before that, living at my parents' house. My chosen family wouldn't care about my fuck-ups, lack of direction, or the PhD project that was already starting to appear doomed to fail. They wouldn't punish me with tense silences, bitter arguments, or underhand criticism loaded in seemingly innocuous pleasantries. My choices wouldn't burden them; unlike my mother, who, while I went to see her at the hospice (as it turned out, my last visit before she died), blurted out: "I just wish I could have seen you *make* something of yourself." Now I would live with people like Otto who didn't care about forging "professional" careers or accruing wealth – both ciphers for conformity, he said (although, as I would discover later, he had done both; made a fortune out of software before turning his back on the whole sordid enterprise). I'd start anew and simply forget what came before. I'd become independent, resolved, fully formed.

Someone had brought down a battery-powered lava lamp and placed it on top of the piano, where it glowed lime green, turning the piano's white keys into acid streaks. Inside the glass chamber, a glob of amorphous goo rose and stretched, pulled apart, divided. Green light rippled across Otto's face; his smile, everything about him appeared generous, vivacious. There was something else, too. The room was full of people and conversation and laughter, but his eyes kept resting on me. I looked away and pretended not to notice. Part of me felt uncomfortable; another part basked in his gaze. Surely this attractive, older, interesting man isn't interested in me, I thought. I glanced over. Our eyes met.

He moved with a confident, rolling gait – almost a prowl – as he stalked out of the room and returned holding a beer, crossed the room and handed it to me without a word, just a look, a sly smile. Seeing that I was shivering, he slipped behind me into the shadows and draped a woollen blanket over my bare shoulders. His fingers brushed my skin, igniting sparks that flew up my neck, making me shudder. He sat on the piano stool opposite and watched me, only me, as though he could eat me up.

After the party was over, the parlour became a storage room once again.

Standing outside the room now, I open the door and peek inside. In the grey morning light, it looks like a garage, filled with sad and abandoned things that don't seem to belong anywhere: a rusted bike Otto had meant to fix for me; stacks of cardboard boxes full of junk; old placards we've taken to protests, brought home and discarded on the floor.

Next, I wander into the sitting room, which is cold and empty, the wood-burning stove unlit. An imprint in the sofa and a blanket balled up in the corner between one arm and a cushion tells me where Otto spent the night. I hear laughter coming from the kitchen. I hesitate before going in; if Otto's in there, I don't know what I'll say to him. As I open the door, I'm greeted by a wave of warmth, the chorus of 'Fairytale of New York' on the radio, the hiss of hot oil, and the deep, sweet scent of caramelised onions. Otto isn't there; Anaïs and Rory are standing together by the hob, Anaïs stirring the onions and laughing as Rory tries to toss a couple of garlic cloves into the pan and misses. "You are such a pro," she says, before they both look round at me at the same time and stop laughing. They seem to relax slightly when they realise it's me who's entered, not Otto.

"Oh, hello," says Anaïs, smiling. "Sorry, I did not realise that you were home."

"Do you know where Otto is?"

"He went out earlier," says Rory. "Didn't say where he was going."

Anaïs and Rory glance at each other quickly. The frying onions fizzle in the pan. 'Wonderful Christmastime' starts playing.

"How are you?" Anaïs asks me.

"Fine," I say. "What are you making?"

"I am trying to make a *jus*. Rory is trying to sabotage it."

"No, I'm not, I'm the perfect sous-chef."

"I have discovered that Rory is extremely xenophobic. He bet me twenty pounds that I could not cook an English

61

roast dinner, certainly not a vegan roast, just because I am French."

"I just meant you'd cook it too well. The point of a traditional roast dinner is tasting as bland and boring as possible."

"Would you like to help, Jade? Or you can just stay and talk with us, if you prefer."

"Yeah, just sit back and watch Anaïs put me to work instead."

"I don't mind helping," I say.

Anaïs offers me a bowl of parsnips to peel. I sit down at the table and start peeling. It's much warmer here than upstairs in Otto's room; condensation drips from the window. The kitchen had been a filthy mess before Anaïs moved in: now it's clean and ordered, the fridge well-stocked. Unicorn Grocery tote bags are stowed neatly inside a wicker box beside the counter, rather than flung under the table as they had been previously. I realise, guiltily, that I've never offered to help with this.

"What are your plans for Christmas?" she asks.

"Not sure. I might end up going to my dad's. Haven't seen him for a while."

Anaïs says she's going back to Provins to stay with her family for a few weeks. She tells us about the town's cobblestone streets and medieval architecture, beautifully decorated every Christmas like something out of a fairy tale. Rory continues chopping celery quietly, no longer smiling. He takes a quick swig from his beer. He leans over and turns the radio off: "Sorry, this music's starting to drive me insane," he mutters.

Anaïs sits beside me and asks, "Is Otto going with you?"

"No. I don't think so."

She's trying to make eye contact with me. I shift uncomfortably in my seat as she observes me intently. Does she see something is different about me? Can she see my real face?

"I wondered if the two of you were having a difficult period at the moment. I think Otto can be a ... what's the word... overbearing?"

"I believe the word you're searching for is 'dickhead'," says Rory. Anaïs kicks him in the leg. She turns her attention back to me.

"Ignore Rory, he's drunk. I hope you do not mind me saying this. I wanted to tell you – if you need to talk to someone – if you need anything – you can talk to us, OK?"

Her eyes are a deep, dark brown, almost black. She smiles kindly and waits for me to speak. I've not experienced an offer of friendship like this for so long, it catches me off-guard. A painful lump forms in the back of my throat. I feel like I might spill everything.

Then I notice the hesitancy in her eyes. The slight shine on them, their glassiness. Even her lovely smile seems awkwardly fixed now, like she's maintaining it only for my benefit.

My skin crawls: something moves and writhes within me, snakelike. I notice again the shapelessness of my hands. I carry Jade's body, but her personal problems don't matter. Not when I belong to Bear. I am sustenance, I am energy, pure and uncomplicated. I don't have to carry Jade much longer. I don't have to feel what she feels.

63

Anaïs looks really concerned now. Her smile has faded. Even Rory is watching me, temporarily distracted from his own troubles.

"Sorry," I say, swallowing the lump in my throat, forcing myself back to the present moment. "Was just thinking." I try to smile. "Thanks, Anaïs. I really am OK though."

I pick up a half-peeled parsnip, willing my fingers to stop trembling. "Here, let me help with dinner." I say, wishing Anaïs would stop staring. After a moment, she seems to accept it. She smiles and says, "Of course. We are here if you need us."

She goes back to her onions and pours in a jug of stock, then turns to Rory and asks, "Why did you turn off the music?"

She switches the radio on and sings along loudly to 'Last Christmas'.

"Oh god, not this song," Rory groans.

They joke and chat and flirt with each other. They try hard not to exclude me, keeping me in the loop of their conversation, but there's no mistaking it: I'm no longer one of them.

vi.

I find Otto sitting on my side of the bed, hunched over, his back to me. He doesn't hear me creep across the carpet, picking my steps carefully through the mess on the floor. I come close enough to see that he's looking through my phone.

"I thought it was mine," he cries, flinging it over my head when I try to grab it out of his hands. It lands on the bed. I snatch it up. "I picked it up by accident."

He must have guessed my passcode. It was probably easy enough to hack – certainly for someone who used to design software. He'd often bragged about having been an "OG 90s hacker", a teen who could've brought down Shell with a few taps of his keyboard, had he thought of it at the time. More recent technology outpaced him: it had irked Otto when, several months earlier, Rory suggested DDoSing Shell, and then Rory had to explain to Otto what DDoSing was. Though clearly Otto still knew a few tricks. Maybe I should be more surprised he hasn't broken into my phone sooner – unless, of course, he has. How naive of me. I press the home screen, the app menu; the most recently opened app was my email.

"If you were serious about not wanting to be together anymore," Otto continues, "you probably wouldn't leave your stuff lying around in my room. You'd be looking for another place to live."

I open the search bar in my email, tap to see the most recent searches: *Alaska.*

"Maybe you're not that serious about leaving after all. You don't seem to have a fucking clue what you want, Jade."

I wonder if Otto's been snooping at other times. The corner of my laptop is poking out under the bath towel I'd dropped on the floor earlier. He could easily hack into it. Maybe he's already tried.

I shove my phone and laptop into a tote bag and storm

out. Smells of roasting potatoes and parsnips waft into the hallway from the kitchen but I race to the door and ignore them, ignore Anaïs calling, "Jade! Dinner is ready!"

Outside the sky is charcoal-black, the air icy. I pull my sleeves down over my balled fists and fold my arms, shivering; I don't have a coat. My bag swings into my side as my legs carry me down to the end of the street, outside the fried chicken takeaway and the off licence. Blue neon lights dazzle me. I stop and just stand there. People bustle out of the shop carrying bottles of wine and cans of lager, chatting and laughing; there are young couples, groups on booze-fuelled nights out. A few of them look at me strangely: the girl with the melted face.

I don't know where I'm going. There's nowhere else to go but back to Otto's – the thought of that makes my stomach drop, my chest tighten. I need a break from there, just for a little while.

I pull out my phone and call Dad, catching him off guard: he was in the middle of reading. We haven't spoken in weeks: not since he phoned to ask how my PhD was coming along and I couldn't give him a definite answer, prompting an argument. He sounds bemused when I ask what he's doing for Christmas. My voice is cheery and false. He agrees to pick me up from Banbury train station, a twenty-minute drive away from his house. The train leaves on Saturday morning, Christmas Eve.

After quietly returning to the house, I pack the night before, making sure to take my laptop. I've already changed the passcode on my phone (to 10416, the date I leave for

Alaska) as well as the password on my computer: I pick a word Otto would never be able to guess. *Ouroboros.* But a former software engineer might still be able to hack into it if he really wants to. The knot in my chest tightens again at the thought of him reading my thesis.

On Saturday morning, I get up early, before everyone else. I creep downstairs, carrying a rucksack on my shoulder that's filled with a week's worth of clothes: I don't know how long I'll be gone exactly. Anaïs's suitcase is packed and ready in the hallway. Otto is asleep on the sofa. We haven't spoken for days; I haven't told him about going to my dad's. I leave without saying goodbye.

vii.

Dad meets me at the station at ten past four, the sun already plunging down the burnt orange sky. He's put on weight since the last time I saw him. His old Regatta raincoat is tight around his middle. We hesitate before putting our arms around each other. My nose is crushed briefly into his shoulder; his paunch presses into my stomach, pushing me away. He pats me firmly on the back like I was an old pal instead of his only daughter.

We walk to the car park in silence and get into the Jeep. Dad's always had a Jeep, even when we'd lived in London and the car's size and power was unnecessary, even ludicrous – now his choice of car finally made some sense (Otto would argue otherwise, had he been here) as we bumped up and down through potholed, winding roads. I wondered if he liked living in this area. Throughout his working life, when we moved from city to city, Dad declared he would spend his retirement in Oxfordshire. How he'd earned it. He'd repeat the tale of his life: coming from Hull fishermen who joked that Hunters had the North Sea in their veins. His father expected him to leave school at sixteen and join them on the boat. But Dad defied my grandfather and went on to do A-levels and an Engineering degree at Durham. As a boy he'd had a penchant for taking things apart and putting them back together. He'd tamper with anything – toasters, microwaves, televisions. He'd surround himself with the guts of mechanical things, the same way his father surrounded himself with fish entrails and vacant eyes. Dad longed to escape the stink of rotten fish, the indignity of Hull. He always told the same story: how he'd yearned for greener pastures.

"How was the train journey?" he asks, breaking the silence between us.

"Fine," I reply. He casts me a sidelong glance, unconvinced.

"You ought to get a car," he says. "I wouldn't have dreamed of not having a car at your age."

I look out of the window. Really? It's started already. I used to bite the inside of my cheek a lot when I was younger. I developed canker sores that made me wince when I ate. I only managed to kick the habit after I left home. Now, after all this time, I find myself squeezing my own flesh between my teeth, my tongue searching the surface of my mouth.

"You don't need a car if you live in a city," I retort. "And I'd have to learn to drive first."

"Twenty-five years old and still not able to drive," he mutters.

For the remainder of the journey, we don't converse with each other, though Dad continues to ramble on as if he's forgotten I'm in the car and is just talking to himself. He cycles through topics: the bad state of the roads, tourists ransacking the area, lazy contractors letting him down. He does not ask my opinion on any topic, nor any further questions. He's oblivious to my deformity. If he had noticed the changes, he would have remarked on them – he is always the first to point out my flaws, those areas requiring improvement. Jade's ghost hovers between us; he can't see through her. He can't see me at all.

The radio is too quiet to hear under the enormous engine's roar, the percussive pops of loose stones on the road, Dad's irate drone. I stare out of the passenger window, watching the wheat fields, patched with snow, go by: a blur of green and white. I feel my phone buzzing in my bag. Must be the tenth time. I ignore it.

Gravel crunches beneath the Jeep's wheels as it crawls over the long driveway, fenced either side by bare trees. I glimpse the house between the skeletal branches and Dad pulls up outside, parking on a bank of clay and stones.

The scene through the car window is bleak. The trees, pond and meadow that were once here for centuries undisturbed had been cleared to make way for Dad's extension and garden. I say "garden" for that's the intention, at least, for this flat expanse of brown earth. It must have rained earlier: workmen's boots have pockmarked the clay and left a thousand tiny puddles. They glow under the vermillion sky like the eyes of a monstrous arachnid.

The nineteenth-century farmhouse had been expanded and adapted to provide all the comforts of modern living: heated floorboards, motion sensor lighting, air conditioning for the torrid weeks of early summer. This was my parents' dream home, their escape to the country envisaged decades ago. Only Mum didn't live long enough to move in. The barn isn't finished yet, Dad reminds me, before grumbling about his incompetent contractors who still haven't found the right parts to complete the guest house kitchen and bathroom suite. For now, I'll have to sleep in the second bedroom in the main house. "As much of an eyesore as ever," says Dad, pointing across the field at the barn, which has looked the same way since renovations began on the property three years ago: rigged with scaffolding, a tip out front. Dad shakes his head. "It's been a nightmare."

We step into the main house. Dad frowns and fusses with the sticking zipper on his coat. When Dad moved in only weeks after Mum died, he quickly found himself contending with the irritations of living in a new home. The fluff of new carpets sticking to clothes. Unwelcome discoveries of shoddy paintwork and botched carpentry. Piles of boxes to unpack. Nothing where you thought it would be, everything taking longer; a pain in the arse just to find a damn hanger or work the new washing machine. The house demanded constant attention, like an overgrown, undisciplined child. It cried for better ventilation in the bathroom and a window sash that didn't jam. Its tantrums blew kitchen spotlights.

Dad goes to the kitchen to make tea. I wait in the hall-way, peering through the open door to the living room: a depressing place, for all its cheerful kitsch cushions and hand-crocheted doilies, its drawings of geese dressed in bonnets and wellies hung on the wall, which Mum thought were just lovely. Most things inside the house were brand new; purchasing them was one of the few times when Dad had been truly extravagant. The curtains, fittings, appliances and furniture had all been carefully selected by my mum, the supreme homemaker, who never had the chance to enjoy any of it.

Dad reappears with a teapot and two cups on a tray and we head into the conservatory. The lamps and ceiling lights turn on automatically. There are no Christmas decorations, no tree – Dad doesn't bother with any of that anymore. In this house it could be any other evening in winter. Dad places the tray on the coffee table and plonks himself into a wicker armchair, groaning with the effort. He'd mentioned something about his knees giving him grief. Besides the tray, the table is cluttered with newspapers, a well-thumbed Winston Churchill biography, his reading glasses. I sit on the sofa opposite. The cushions are stiff, still not worn in.

I ask how much work is left to do in the barn. He lists off a couple of things before trailing off. He seems to have lost interest in the topic. He picks up his glasses and today's newspaper off the pile, flicks through a couple of pages, tosses it back down. Then he shuffles in his chair, uncrosses and re-crosses his legs, clears his throat.

"So, what's the plan then, after you've finished your doctorate?" he asks. I'm more bothered by the flippant tone of his voice than the question itself. The hint of sarcasm, as though we both already know I have no plan.

I had expected the conversation to turn to my future prospects. It always does. Some remnant of Jade – whatever is left of her – wants to tell him whatever he wants to hear. Feels sorry for him. Understands his need to guide his daughter, to have some control in this empty, too-large house.

"I was thinking of travelling for a while," I reply, toying with the idea of telling him about the conference.

"You're not going to be a lecturer?" He takes off his glasses and wipes the lenses with the bottom of his cardigan.

I lean forward on my seat, unable to sink back into the cushions.

"I don't think so."

He sighs and shakes his head, chuckling drily. He flings his glasses onto the table. The smile creeping across his face is thin, insincere. I read the calculation in his face: he's preparing to give me another dressing-down, not for his own benefit but out of absolute necessity, since apparently whenever he tries to explain this sort of thing to me it goes in one ear and out the other. Anxiety boils up in the pit of my stomach. Fight, flight or freeze? In the wild there's only a split second to decide. I feel my defences and counter arguments rising like the hairs on the back of my neck.

"What's the point of doing the PhD, then?" he asks, bitterly.

"There doesn't have to be a point."

"Well, why are you doing it?"

"Because it's interesting."

"But what will that lead to?"

"I don't know yet."

The wicker chair creaks as Dad leans forward. My heart is racing. My shapeless hands are shaking. In spite of my transformation, all the old feelings are resurging.

"You need to decide," he says.

He isn't laughing or smiling now. This isn't a joking matter.

"You need to think very carefully," he goes on. "You don't want to be living in that bedsit forever."

"House share."

"Living like that simply isn't acceptable. You need your own house, a car, a real job. Something worthwhile, lucrative. A professional career..."

I let the words wash over me, soaking and heavy, like being drenched in dirty water from a puddle splashed again and again by the same reckless driver. I'd heard it all before, in one form or another. How I was ruining my life. I should have known this visit was a bad idea. And yet it was the first thing I thought of as a means to get away from Otto.

I had imagined that, somehow, this visit would be different – that Dad would be pleased to see me; our conversations would be warm and affectionate; he would kiss my forehead and tell me he was proud of me, that I was doing just fine, there was no need to worry. I thought, somehow, he'd intuit this was to be the last time we'd see each other. Then again, by turning all of our conversations towards my future, perhaps Dad has always foreseen some impending doom. In all of us there is an innate alertness for shifting fates: our ancestors looked to the sky for omens and auspices, read the position of the stars, the red dawn. We may experience a bad feeling about something, sense seismic changes about to occur. Hear the hum of the earth. Feel the presence of God.

I love you, I could tell him. *I miss Mum too*. He's still monologuing; he doesn't pause long enough for me to speak. There was so much Jade had wanted to say to him and never did. I suppose none of that matters anymore. When he finally tails off, I have nothing left to say.

Dad announces it's suppertime and disappears, returning after a couple of minutes with two plates of cheese and crackers. He's either forgotten or chosen to ignore that I don't eat dairy. He switches on the TV, which I can barely hear over the sound of him munching. The evening wears on. I feel tired, weakened: I want to crawl upstairs, hibernate, wake up in the spring. Everything will be different by then.

The lights come on as I go upstairs. I don't go straight to the guest room. I enter Dad's bedroom, what would have been Mum's bedroom too, had she lived a little longer. My mum. I have trouble picturing her face. I have barely any memories of her. Those that come to mind seem false, trite inventions rather than things that actually happened. Is that because it's still too soon after her death? Or because I didn't really know her. She was a passenger in my life: we found ourselves in the same carriage, briefly, and then she alighted.

74

The only thing I remember with absolute clarity is the day she died. I arrived at the hospice too late: she'd already sunk into sleep. She didn't open her eyes or respond when I leaned over her and told her it was me, I was here. I took a seat next to Dad beside her bed. I'd been to see her every couple of weeks during those final months, spending more time with her than I had in years. I thought it would mend things somehow, finally bring us closer. Instead, our conversations have been stilted, skimming the surface of our relationship and disregarding the murky leagues of resentments beneath. It was a relief: neither of us wanted to delve any deeper. She didn't have the energy and I didn't have the courage – not when I saw her. Her body was shrunken, her arms too thin, the skin on them loose and papery. She told me she hadn't eaten a full meal for weeks, she had no appetite left.

Hours passed. Now and then, quiet sobs escaped her throat, though when Dad or I rose to check, she was still only sleeping. Death came on gradually, almost orgasmically: the sobs came back but suddenly her eyes were half-open, staring into nothingness. Her mouth fell open; her bared teeth were strangely white against her rapidly greying skin. Dad put his hands around her face. I couldn't touch her. Seconds elongated as she fell silent and still. I didn't cry. I had witnessed something sublime happening to a woman I had little to do with, besides her being my mother. I stood back and looked at her gaping mouth, wondering why her mouth had opened like that.

I find myself rifling through Dad's wardrobe. Would he

have kept anything of hers? He wasn't a sentimental man. But I discover a stash of Mum's clothes hung at the end of the rack. They smell of her perfume: lemon and jasmine. She liked light, delicate, fresh-smelling things. I touch her dresses, scarves, jumpers – and yes, her coats. Here it is: her prized mink coat. The softest black fur except for several patchy, cropped areas where she'd tried to cut out red acrylic spatters. She never wore it out but couldn't bring herself to throw it away either. She didn't buy a new one; I don't think Dad ever offered to replace it. He wasn't frivolous with his money. He'd splashed out for their wedding anniversary but after the day had passed, I think the gesture must have seemed pointless to him. Or maybe he had offered to replace it but for whatever reason she turned him down. I don't know. I never asked her. Maybe she was afraid I'd subject a replacement to the same vandalism. She didn't want another beautiful thing to be destroyed.

I run my hands over the smooth, glossy sleeves. I pull the coat off the hanger and put it on. Wearing fur, I feel bigger than myself. Majestic. This is what Bear must feel like. I hug the lapels to my chest, close my eyes, breathe in deeply. The lingering perfume has disappeared, replaced with rich, deep, earthy smells. Moss and mushrooms. Rain-soaked soil. Sweet, dark secretions of decomposing matter. A predator's musk: the remnants of bone, blood and rotting flesh caught in its fur. Between my fingers I squeeze thick black tufts, grown several inches longer since I put the coat on. It's not mink fur anymore.

It's my bear hide.

viii.

Otto has left thirty-six missed calls, seven voicemail messages, forty-five texts.

The final one reads: *I'm truly sorry for breaking into your phone. Please come home.*

Dad gives me a lift to the train station the day after New Year's Day. I breathe a little easier once the car pulls out of the driveway and the house recedes behind us, even though I'm heading back to Otto's. I was starting to feel too much like Jade again. Apart from when I put on the coat. Dad doesn't notice the bulge in my rucksack that wasn't there on my journey down.

From: Fairy Tales, Fables & Folklore Symposium <[email address redacted]>
Sent: 03 January 2016 14:52
To: Jade Hunter <[email address redacted]>
Subject: FFF Symposium 2016

Dear Jade,

I am delighted to inform you that your paper proposal has been accepted for presentation at the 4th Global Symposium on Fairy Tales, Fables and Folklore, which will take place at University of Alaska Fairbanks from Monday 11th – Friday 15th April 2016.[14] You will find important information about registration, deadlines and accommodation, etc., in the attached letter.

We received over 300 fascinating proposals from all over the world but were only able to accept 180 people on the sympo-

---

14 Editor's note: I am grateful to the FFF Symposium organisers, who kindly provided Jade's abstract entitled, 'Beast, lover, doppelgänger: the bear and its relationship to women in fairy tales and folklore', which she originally submitted on November 30, 2015 (see Appendix). The full text of this paper is lost or perhaps never existed to begin with, if Jade chose not to write it (likely the case, given her ulterior motive for accepting her invitation to the conference in Alaska). Only the original abstract is extant. If Jade had chosen to write the full paper, it would have been saved on her laptop. However, Jade's laptop was never found among the possessions left in the hotel room where she checked in on her first night in College. Therefore, we must surmise it was lost, stolen or destroyed, possibly by Jade herself. Assuming Jade wrote the paper, she may have saved a backup copy (or shared it with someone else via email, as she did with her "thesis"); if so, it has never been traced.

sium programme, with many people on a waiting list. We would be grateful if you could confirm your attendance by replying to this email as soon as possible, please, so that if you cannot attend, we can give your place to someone on the waiting list in good time for them to make the necessary arrangements for travel and accommodation.

If you have any queries, please contact us at [email redacted] We look forward to seeing you at the symposium.

Best wishes,

Freyja

CHAPTER THREE
Berserker

Berserkers (literally: "bear shirt wearers") were
Norse warriors who wore bear hides into battle.
Legend has it that when the warriors donned the
hides, they actually transformed into bears. It is said
their appearance was so fearsome to their opponents
that men would flee the battlefield in terror.

H. Castelli, "Bear worship in Ancient Scandinavia",
Anthropology Review (2011)[15]

i.

Otto and I settle into an uneasy truce. When I return to
the house – strangely vacant, with Anaïs still in France

---

15 Editor's note: The above quote does not appear in any issue of *Anthropology Review* – nor any other journal or book that I could find – and
while there is an anthropologist named H. Castelli, she has confirmed
that she never authored this article. However, the information within
the quote is corroborated by numerous sources. As with other published
material from which Jade directly quotes, the source text is either lost,
misquoted, or misattributed, or it may be her fabrication.

and Rory gone to Edinburgh for Hogmanay – Otto's bedroom is waiting for me, tidied up; the heaps of dirty laundry and splayed-open books and screwed up, used tissues are gone. He says he's "giving me space": an expression he doesn't believe in but thinks will appease me. The temporariness of this measure is implicit; he expects I will soon cool off, take him back. He's moved into the sitting room, sleeping on the sofa under a heap of moth-eaten blankets. He doesn't bother lighting the stove, despite how cold it is. The log basket is empty. Out in the garden, piles of broken fencing and wooden crates lie coated in frost, abandoned. I spot a small gardening fork leaning against a cracked, upside-down terracotta plant pot: the fork's long tines give me an idea. When Otto's away one day, I creep into the garden and take it, secreting it for later.

I spend most of the time in Otto's bedroom, wearing the fur coat and sitting under the duvet to keep warm.

He could serve notice and evict me or just kick me out – there's no tenancy contract for him to violate, so I'm entirely subject to his whims. He doesn't do either. My excursion over Christmas must have panicked him. He keeps out of my way, mostly, exchanging a few words with me in the kitchen. Polite questions about how I'm doing, how my dad's doing – his concern about my dad is obviously fake, designed to soften me up. His easy smile is a mask for his rage. Sometimes I catch him watching me. I don't know what he's looking for or if he notices something different about me. I give nothing away: my smooth new face is blank as ever. We're two animals living in the same cage, keeping our distance, wary of each other, claws poised for attack. He watches me from the sitting room as I pass through the hallway. I can't read his expression. What does it mean? Fear? Loathing? Hunger?

I am not his to consume.

ii.

There are days when I don't think I can go through with it. When I can feel my resolve faltering. Now that I've accepted my place at the conference and applied for funding from the university to pay for my plane ticket, it's all becoming real, not the idle fantasy I've been obsessing over for weeks. The thought of what's coming sparks an electric current under my skin. Just the words 'April' and 'Alaska' can send me into a fit of laughter. But sometimes when I think about that final day, when I will give up my body, creeping closer, terror eclipses my excitement like a dark cloud over the sun.

I must renounce all such claims to selfhood.

When I hear the slam of the front door, the sound of Otto going out, I gather them up. My degree certificates. Tutor feedback on my essays. Love letters from Otto. Crumpled shopping receipts fished from pockets and bags. Old train tickets. A Moleskine journal (a Christmas gift from Anaïs). Spiral notebooks and A4 pads. Pages and pages of lecture notes, essay notes, thesis notes. All the pieces of paper that made up a life. I set aside a printout of my plane ticket, my passport, banknotes; I'll need those later. I carry the rest downstairs to the sitting room and drop them on the floor.

I light the stove. Its cast iron belly bursts into flame, rumbling with hunger.

I fling my degree certificates into the inferno. They curl at the edges, burst in the middle with bright orange heat, turn brown and then black. I gather courage from this. Toss in Otto's love letters. Tear out pages of notebooks, scrunch them up by the handful. When the fire is sated, a soft and even kindle, I feed it the final scraps: receipts, train tickets. Somehow burning these makes me saddest: these small, mundane, familiar things that we rely on briefly. I remember packing up Mum's toothbrush and underwear at the hospice. Then realising no one would ever use those items again.

I warm my hands by the fire until the papers blacken, dim to embers. Everything around me is dark; the sun set while I was burning. Vision blitzed by staring so long at the flames, I can't make out the shape of the sofa or the outline of the door. It's as though the fire swallowed it all, leaving nothing left. Except for my body.

iii.

Dad calls me a couple of weeks into January. At first, I think he'll ask where the coat is. I'm wearing it when he calls.

"Have you thought any more about what we talked about?" he asks after a perfunctory greeting. Apparently he either hasn't noticed the coat's missing or it's not his chief concern.

"What *we* talked about?"

"At Christmas," he says, impatiently. "When we discussed what you're going to do after university."

"I'm going to Alaska."

"Alaska?"

"At the end of April."

"What on earth for?"

"A conference."

"I thought you weren't going to bother becoming an academic."

"I'm not."

"Then why are you going?"

"It should be a transformative experience."

He sighs deeply. "I've told you, you should really be thinking about your career. We always used to have a couple of interns in the office around Easter. They might still be offering internships this year."

"That sounds terrible, Dad."

"Fine, do something else then," he snaps. "Instead of wasting your time with a pointless PhD without the foggiest idea what you'll do next. No ambition. Living in a bedsit with that waster who's turned you into a communist and a vegan and God knows what else."

I want to laugh but I can't; as he speaks, a familiar mixture of anger and confusion and shame rises up in my body and compacts together at the top of my windpipe, lodging there. My throat becomes sore and tight.

"What really hurts me, Jade," he continues, his voice breaking, "is that you've done so little to help me since your mum died. Apart from Christmas, you never come to see me. You rarely pick up the phone. My only child."

I've only witnessed my dad cry once before, that last time in the hospice. The effect is shocking; I shake as though I have a fever. I choke out the words:

"I don't think I'll see you again before I go to Alaska."

"Well, that's up to you."

"I'm sorry for disappointing you, Dad," I whisper. "But I'll be gone soon."

"What's that? I can't hear you properly."

"I need to go."

I hang up.

Still shivering, I pull the coat tightly around me and crawl into bed, my nest, where I'm cradled in warmth. None of this matters, I tell myself. Pain doesn't last. Pain is part of transformation. Pain will bring me closer to Bear. The fur shields me from the rest of the world, Otto's heavy footsteps downstairs, my memory of Dad's voice.

iv.

My ritual: run a cold bath. Ease gradually in. First toes, then a whole foot, a leg – each part scalds with icy pain, settling after a while into a prickling numbness. The gummed-up shampoo bottles, rusting taps and mildewed tiles disappear. This porcelain shell breaks apart, and I flow with the river.

I am no longer bipedal, anthropoid. Devolving feels so easy, more natural than evolution. Backwards I go: scaled, silver, eyes turned sideways.

I wriggle, I writhe. I am supple and finned. Bubbles escape my gaping mouth. Rushing water explodes in my ears. My goal is to swim upstream, against the current.

I live to feed, to die and provide nutrients for the algae that breathe life and minerals back into the water, or for the beasts prowling on the shore. Nothing about me is wasted or superfluous. Bear waits for me at the surface, paws poised to grab.

Now – now – press the tines of the garden fork into my belly. Pierce skin. Delicious pain. Don't push too far in – just enough to feel the metal turn into claws. To picture Bear scooping my body up, throwing me into his jaws. I slide in bits down his throat, splash into another pool.

The water feels warmer now.

v.

January dies and February is born. February ages and curses March, its soon-to-be successor. The weather's getting warmer. Otto's hovering around me more and more. "This is getting ridiculous," he says, when again I tell him I don't want to go back to sharing a bed. "How many times do I have to apologise? You're being selfish. This is *my* house." Still, he stays on the sofa. He doesn't force me out, although he derides my bourgeois mindset. I lord over the top floor, lady of the house, while he lurks at the bottom, servile and mutinous.

Otto snaps at everyone. He loses his temper over the smallest things – someone forgetting to turn a light off or using up the last of the oat milk. Rory and Anaïs stay out of his way. She casts me a sympathetic glance when we pass each other on the landing. She seems about to speak until we hear Otto stomping upstairs.

On the bad days I seriously consider talking to her, remembering her concern for me before Christmas. I picture myself knocking on her door, being invited in and offered her bed to sit on, her listening to me and offering comforting phrases. But I know I can't tell her the truth. She'd never understand. We don't speak the same language: hers is human, all too human. If I show her what I really am, it will terrify her. She'd wish she never reached out.

vi.

I'm heading downstairs when I hear shouting.

"So, you've given up?"

Otto's voice. I creep across the landing and peer over the banister. In the hallway, Anaïs and Rory are standing together, facing Otto. Anaïs looks distressed, Rory furious. Otto's back is to me, I can't see his face.

"For me, it's not possible," says Anaïs, in her soft, measured way, though I hear a faint tremor in her voice. Rory rests one hand on her shoulder. "Please believe me," she goes on, "I want to help, but I can't risk getting arrested. I could get deported."

"If you cared enough, you'd take that risk."

"It's not the same risk for you as it is for her, though, is it," Rory interjects, glaring at Otto.

"Don't you start with me."

"It's not Anaïs's fault they're so hard-line on protesters."

"They're hard-line because they're afraid of us. That's why we have to keep trying."

"Otto, how many protests have I done with you? None of them ever change a fucking thing."

"We have a mission."

"Would you get over the fucking superhero complex."

"Rory..." Anais warns.

"Get over the tortured alcoholic act," Otto retorts.

Anaïs squeezes Rory's arm but he doesn't let up. "When are you going to stop acting as though you're our leader? So what if we don't want to come to the protest this time? It's our choice."

"You're all in it together, aren't you? You, Anaïs and Jade. You've got this tight little circle behind my back."

"What are you talking about? This has got nothing to do with Jade."

I retreat from the banister, looking down at them from a little further behind the wall.

"She hasn't been herself for months, and now I know why."

"I think that's got more to do with you being her boy-friend."

"Rory, stop –"

"When Jade moved in, I thought she was just someone else you'd recruited for the group, but then you couldn't keep her hands off her. What's the age difference again, fifteen years?"

"The age thing doesn't matter to us. You and Anaïs are the same age, but I don't think she wants you pawing her."

Rory withdraws his hand from Anaïs's shoulder as though it had turned red hot. Anaïs traipses away and slumps onto the bottom stair, her head in her hands.

"Anaïs and I are just friends."

"Bullshit."

"You can't talk shit about anyone. You're old as fuck and you're with a twenty-five-year-old. But it makes sense you wanting a much younger girlfriend, given how much you like telling people what to do."

"I want you out of my house by tomorrow morning. Both of you."

"Fine by me."

"Otto, please," says Anaïs, no longer trying to conceal her voice trembling.

Otto squares up to Anaïs. "I saw what you wrote in that little Christmas card you left for Jade. 'Here if you need to talk.' What might you two be talking about? What's she been telling you?"

"She hasn't told me anything," says Anaïs, sounding surprised.

What card, I wonder. When I returned after Christmas, I'd found her gift – a bag labelled "Joyeux Noël, Jade! Je

90

t'embrasse, Anaïs" and containing the Moleskine journal –
on the kitchen table but nothing else.

Rory inserts himself in front of Otto, sputtering, "Leave
her alone."

"You've been poisoning Jade against me," Otto says.

"I am worrying about Jade too, Otto," Anaïs says, a
pleading tone in her voice. "That is why I wrote the card."

"She's my girlfriend," says Otto, "I'm the one who's looking out for her. I want you to leave by tomorrow. You don't
live here anymore."

"Come on, Anaïs," Rory mutters, offering a hand to lift
her up. "Let's go and pack our stuff. It's all for the best,
really. We can finally get away from this prick."

They begin to walk upstairs. I quickly tiptoe up to the
bedroom, hearing the sitting room door slam behind Otto.

vii.

There are more echoes in the house now, two rooms emp-
tier. I move my things into Anaïs's room. Otto leans against
the doorframe, watching me place my books on the desk.

"You can have your room back now," I say, stacking
another armful of books.

"I didn't ask for it back."

He walks over and touches my sleeve. I pull away. He
reaches for my sleeve again, looks me up and down, feels
the coat, pinches the fur.

"Why are you always wearing this?"

"It was my mum's."

His expression hardens. "Is it real fur?" he asks. I don't answer. I try to get to the empty wardrobe to hang up my clothes but he stands in my way.

"She gave it to you?"

"I took it from my dad's at Christmas."

"You feel comfortable wearing that, do you?" he scoffs, his eyes gleaming with contempt. "The skin of a murdered animal?" He tugs one of the lapels. "Take it off, it's disgusting."

"No, I won't. It's mine."

He yanks the bottom of one sleeve, trying to slip it down off my arm. I pull away and cross my arms tight against my chest, struggling as he tries to pry them apart. He wraps himself around me from behind, trying to wrestle the coat off me that way.

"Take... it... off!"

His arms squeeze me like the teeth of a steel trap. I push against them, screaming, desperate to escape their terrible strength. One of his hands slides up my chest and neck towards my face, covering my mouth – I catch it between my teeth, bite down as hard as I can.

A cry from behind me, pain mingled with fury. He lets go.

"What the fuck?"

He backs out of the room, clutching his bleeding hand with the other. He's shaking, glaring at me.

Curiously, I feel much calmer. Whatever doubts I had fade away: it's working the way I thought it would, this sequence of transformations, falling into each other like dominoes. First, the mink fur became a bear hide, the way wine can become blood. Now the coat is channelling Bear's strength. I smile at the strange and wonderful alchemy of this transference of energy.

"Do you think this is funny?"

I look up at Otto. I'd forgotten he was still there.

"I'm transforming," I say, simply. There's no need to hide the truth anymore.

"There's something seriously wrong with you. I don't know who you are anymore."

He leaves, finally. I breathe deeply, cleansed by waves of purifying energy emanating from every fibre of the coat, feeling Bear's closeness.

viii.

On the 1st of April, everything feels warmer, brighter. Otto patrols the house, keeping track of my comings and goings.

I cross the days off in my head. I count them down like a child waiting for Christmas. Two weeks left. One week left.

The night before, I wake up, some ancient sense of danger rousing me from sleep. I feel it before I see it: a tall silhouette in the dark.

Otto slumps onto the end of the bed. I smell alcohol on him.

"Please don't go. Don't go," he slurs.

I say nothing. I check my phone for the time: 3:09 AM. The taxi will arrive to take me to the airport at four-thirty.

I fly out at seven.

"I thought you loved me," he says.

He lies down next to me and I steel myself, waiting to pounce if he so much as touches me. He starts snoring. Relief washes over me. I might as well get up now, get ready, finish packing, wait for the taxi to arrive. I'm wide awake.

CONCLUSION

Katabasis

A boat is carrying me along a river through a cave.

The roof is ridged like a mouth; its breath smells of rot, bile. Stalactites drip down like huge drops of frozen saliva. Guttural rumbles reverberate from deep within. Under the flickering lamp hanging from the stern, I can see only what's immediately around me: darkly churning water, the cave's walls, the crude metal vessel carrying me (won't it rust? won't it sink?). On narrow shores on either side of the river, piles of bones are revealed: bear skeletons, hundreds of thousands of years old, bathed in shadow and dust. I can't see what lies ahead. The cave might stretch miles further. Or I might have already reached the end.

I listen to the lapping river, to the cave's deep echoes. A voice calls to me distantly. It could be Mum's voice. It could be an animal's cry.

Something shakes me awake. Turbulence. I open my eyes and find myself sitting in a plane. My ears are awash with the roar of turbines, the ping of a bell alerting passengers to fasten their seatbelts. I look out the window. Beneath

95

wisps of cloud, jagged teeth of mountain peaks appear, their white coating underscored by crags, evergreen and scrub, by the curving paths of rivers. Settlements are dotted here and there, but mostly it's wild terrain as far as I can see. Snow stretches to the horizon and glows amber under the falling sun.

The passenger next to me is crunching her way through a bag of crackers and watching a film on the tiny screen on the back of the seat in front. The man on her other side picks up the crackling plastic cup off his tray and drains its final dregs of red wine.

The pilot announces we'll be landing soon. My belly sinks and turns with the plane as it begins its descent.

The journey's almost over. There's a new buzz in the air: restless excitement overtakes the passengers. I feel it too.

So much time and preparation went into this ritual. All that remains is the sacrifice. The feast.

Part Two

Part Two

Ursula was declared guilty of Jade's murder on March 15, 2017, exactly one year and eleven months after Jade was reported missing.

Later that year, I began a series of interviews with Ursula in prison in order to hear her side of the story regarding what happened in those first weeks after Jade's disappearance. Although she requested that the content of these interviews would not be quoted from directly – after all, quotes from her journals had been weaponised against her in the trial – I am grateful for her permission to paraphrase or faithfully interpret her version of the events as she described them to me.

What follows takes place from April 15 until May 1, 2016.

The black cloud arched like a church window. It framed Bear Mountain in the east, its darkness standing out against the snow on the mountain peak. The cloud appeared out of nowhere last week and seemed to stretch a little further across the sky with each passing day. Over the valley, it cast a shadow that pointed across the treetops and slowly approached the cabin. Ursula leaned on her axe and wondered what it meant: a thunderstorm, or the eruption of nuclear war? *Whatever happens, I'll be ready*, she thought. A pile of cleanly chopped logs lay at her boots. Her arms were sore from holding up the axe and striking it hard through the wood on the block. Her body got tired a lot quicker these days. She rolled her shoulders, inhaled deeply, and lifted the axe. She had to push on. There was still so much to do.

During the rest of the morning, Ursula collected the firewood and loaded it into the cabin, emptied the toilet bowl into the compost, and cleaned the solar panels, which she was now able to use again to charge the generator. Up here, the seasons were ruthlessly long: summers of perpetual daylight, winters with almost no daylight at all. Spring had arrived early this year: the ice had already broken up on the Tanana River; starving bears were emerging from hibernation. The sun rose a little earlier each morning, the days were getting brighter and longer – at least, that was until the black cloud appeared, and now the days seemed to be darkening again.

Trees trembled in the unusually warm wind as Ursula climbed through the forest, gripping branches for support. If she lost her balance and fell on the steep slopes, she would probably die. There was nobody left at home to wonder where she'd got to. The last thing she'd see would be eagles watching her up in the trees. Afterwards they would fight each other over scraps of her corpse. The forest had one simple law: eat or get eaten. In the civilised world, however, you waited around to die. If she were unlucky, a rambler might stumble across her bruised, unconscious body; she would wake up twenty miles away in the Fairbanks Memorial Hospital ER, wearing a cotton nightgown like an old lady, her arm attached to a drip. She would have no visitors besides a boy in a white coat with a clipboard and an official badge – they always had badges, these smarter-than-thou types – telling her that no, it was just not possible, she couldn't go home, and would she consider how much more comfortable she would be in a retirement community.

Ursula came to a tree where she'd set a trap, one of ten along the trapline she ran in this acre of forest. A dead squirrel hung by its neck on the snare, its body and tail dangling, swaying slowly in the breeze. She held its body as she clipped the wire that had formed a noose around its neck. After cutting it loose, she inspected her catch. Its head hung limply from its neck, and she could feel the delicate ribcage through its fur. Its eyes were closed slits while its mouth gaped, teeth bared. *No*, she thought, *I will not die in a nursing home – a glorified prison for the decrepit.* Her knees creaked as she began her hike back home with the squirrel tied by its tail to her belt. It swung gently against her thigh as she walked, while her rifle pressed firm and reassuring against her back.

The orange sun began to sink behind the trees as Ursula sat on the sofa, a plate of fried squirrel on her lap. Every evening she sat in the same spot on the sofa, next to the sideboard. The sideboard was topped with framed photographs of Bill and Jake and an illustration of Jesus Christ. At the centre was her favourite photo, the one she had taken of Bill and twelve-year-old Jake, grinning as they kneeled over an enormous grey wolf sprawled at their feet. Looking at the photo made Ursula smile as she finished her meal and licked the grease off her fingers. Mounted on the wall on a wooden plinth was the wolf's head. It bore its long teeth in a ferocious snarl as though it was ready to pounce. She remembered that Bill had enjoyed giving the wolf this expression when he stuffed it. He had been so proud of Jake's first kill, a bald eagle, that he'd stuffed that too. The eagle had beady yellow eyes and was perched in a glass cabinet on the right-hand side of the sideboard, next to the photo of Jake wearing his army uniform. He wasn't a grinning boy in this photo; he was trying on a man's expression, serious and grave. He took after his father: eager to prove himself, his worth as a man, as an American. Bill used to laugh at the irony of this. "A nation of immigrants," he said. "My mother's people were here before any of them. And yet we're treated like outsiders." He'd told her stories about his early childhood in Fairbanks, when there were still segregated schools and movie theatres, notices in restaurant windows that read "No Natives Allowed". Even after that became illegal, plenty of shopkeepers would take one look at young Bill and his mother and refuse to serve them. Ursula's own family disowned her when she ran off with Bill. Not that she cared if she never heard from her father again. Though being cut off from her mother had been hard; there were times when she'd longed for her mother's guidance, her soothing words.

She hated the sight of the uniform, but it was her last photo of Jake, so she kept it and glanced at it often. To remind herself why she stayed here, even though Bill was gone too. It was safer to keep to herself. Look at what the government had cost her family when they persuaded Jake to go and perform his duty to his country – or so they put it. Her Jake, her baby, went off to war – he was only twenty-three – and a year later, two uniformed officers turned up on their doorstep (Bill refused to invite them in) to tell them their son was missing in action, presumed dead. Bill yelled at the officers to get off his property, that Jake's death was their fault; meanwhile Ursula turned the word "missing" over and over in her mind. She decided she would continue to keep Jake's bedroom exactly as he'd left it, hoping someday, somehow, he might return.

Bill wasn't the same man after that. For some years they both went about their daily lives more or less as before, working together as partners, stocking supplies, hunting, repairing the house as it coped with snowstorms in the brutal winters. But his priorities changed. He was more withdrawn. He became easily distracted, reckless.

"I'm going hunting," he announced one day. He told her he would find the biggest black bear, the alpha male. The next morning, he left for the woods to search for tracks: footprints, tufts of fur caught on briars. He journeyed miles through the trees and scaled Bear Mountain. It was June, when the sun shone through the night; he was gone for days at a time, often not stopping to rest. He came home exhausted but could not sleep.

It went like that for weeks. He still hadn't managed to hunt down the bear. She urged him to be careful, even though she knew Bill was a skilled hunter, that he had always taken great care amid the risks and dangers of their way of life. Something felt off as, once again, early one morning – the day of the summer solstice – she watched him storm back into the woods, glimpsing his red plaid shirt between branches one last time before the trees swallowed him.

She waited up all night. He didn't come home.

She knew something wasn't right this time. The next day, and for three days after that, she traced his steps, searching for signs of him but finding none. He wouldn't have been the first person to simply disappear in these woods: the area was known for such cases. But Ursula thought it impossible for Bill to get himself lost. He knew these woods like he knew her face – both were familiar, beloved, home. The woods, however, had turned on him. Creatures known and unknowable lurked there, biding their time, looking for prey. There were wolves. Man-eating spirits. The mythical Land Otter Men, who mimicked the cries of humans to lure the lost. And, of course, there were bears.

Eventually, the woods relinquished what was left of him.

Ursula poured herself another glass of Last Frontier whiskey and watched the shadows slowly swallow the photos until she could no longer see the faces of Bill, Jake and Jesus. She looked out of the window at the night sky and hoped that the Aurora Borealis would appear. Sure enough, a band of shimmering green light materialised out of the blackness. She had heard somewhere that the lights were departed souls dancing, sending a message to the living that they were happy and okay. The green light shone through the window and onto the wolf head and the eagle in the glass cabinet. The stuffed eagle seemed to ruffle its feathers under the flickering light; the wolf's eyes became glowing green pools. At this point Ursula sat up straighter, ignoring her slight dizziness as the room began to spin. This is what she had been waiting for – to resume the conversation.

"That weird black cloud. What does it mean?" she asked. Her tongue felt heavy; her voice came out slurred.

The wolf blinked its bright green eyes. It opened its jaws and Bill's voice came out. "Something bad is coming," it said.

"What's coming?"

"You need to stay strong."

"I'm trying, but it's hard. It's getting harder every day. I need you."

"You must protect yourself."

"*You* didn't. Why did you have to go after that bear?"

But the green light guttered out of the wolf's eyes, and it said no more.

She heard the eagle click its beak. She turned her attention to it and looked into its beady eyes, which stared right back.

"Don't you look at me like that, young man," she said, rubbing tears off her cheeks with her fists. "You shouldn't have gone away either," she added bitterly.

"I had to leave," said the eagle in Jake's voice.

"You didn't. I've told you before. Family's supposed to look out for each other. Your family was here. Not Iraq. The government lied to you. They enslaved you."

The eagle's feathers rose and fell.

"Mother," it said.

In spite of herself, Ursula softened. The eagle did not take its glowing eyes off her. She put her glass down and bent forward, gripping the edge of her seat.

"It's started, hasn't it? Armageddon."

The eagle clicked its beak impatiently.

"Mother, listen. You're running out of time. You'll need to make a choice."

"How do you know all this? Did God send you?"

"You're asking the wrong questions."

She bit her lip, tried to think, but her thoughts were

hazy from the whiskey. She pointed to the glass encasing the eagle. "Are you trapped in there?"

"I was trapped when I was human. Now I'm free." It spoke in a strange, wavering mixture of a man's voice and a boy's.

"Where are you?"

"Anywhere. Nowhere."

Its yellow-green eyes faded to black.

Ursula got up and walked over to the window, a little unsteady on her feet although the room had stopped spinning. The green lights had disappeared from the sky; already it was growing lighter. The dark hours at night would not last much longer. Soon the days would be so long that she would no longer be able to see the Aurora Borealis, and her night-time conversations would end. She dreaded this, even though the green lights did not look like dancing souls to Ursula, but spirits writhing in pain, imprisoned under the dome of the sky.

Ursula was skinning a lynx when she heard a low rumbling sound coming from outside. She put her knife down on the block, hurriedly rinsed the blood off her hands and shook them dry as she went to the window to see what was going on. She was stunned to see the small speck of a car weaving around the hills, coming closer. The rumbling was its engine struggling to contend with the melting snow and its tyres falling into the deep potholes on the road leading to her cabin. Ursula saw that it was a police car.

She went over to the gun rack, took her Ruger .44 Magnum and tucked it under the waistband of her jeans. When she heard the car grind to a halt on her driveway, she waited behind the front door and watched through the glass spyhole. Two troopers got out of the car they'd parked next to her truck. Both men looked up at the yellow flag hanging on a ten-foot pole beside the truck; the breeze caught the fabric, which unfurled and revealed a coiled rattlesnake and the inscription: DONT TREAD ON ME. One of the men waited by the car while the other strode to the door. Ursula waited for the knock before she opened the door a crack, concealing her right hand behind her back, fingers resting on the grip of her gun.

"Yeah? What?"

Ursula guessed the clean-shaven man on her doorstep was about forty. He wore a navy Stetson and a thick fleeced overcoat over his blue uniform. When she opened the door, his facial expression was impassive, though she noticed his eyes flitting behind her, as though he was curious to see inside her home.

"Ma'am, my name is Sergeant Paul Mathers, and this is Trooper Frank Sweeney." He gestured behind him to the other cop, a younger man wearing a hat with earflaps, who leaned on the police car and stared with narrowed eyes at the yellow flag.

"What are you doing on my property?" she demanded.

Mathers blinked, clearly taken aback. Carefully, Ursula pressed her fingers tighter around the grip.

"Is your husband home?" he asked, eyes darting again to

get a look inside.

"No, he is not."

"Ma'am," said Mathers, hooking his thumbs behind his belt, where his own gun hung in its black leather holster, "we're here because of the missing girl. I'm sure you'll have seen the news."

"I don't have a TV."

"Really? Well, a girl's gone missing. A young woman, I should say. Her name is Jade Hunter. Twenty-five years old. Skinny, long black hair, about five foot four. She has a tattoo on her wrist, some kind of symbol, like a snake eating its own tail? Anyway, she's a British student. She'd been staying in a hotel near the college campus. Only she left the hotel on Monday and no one's –"

"There's no one here," she interrupted.

"Ma'am, please, if you'd just listen."

The way he kept saying *ma'am* annoyed Ursula. As though she were stupid; a stupid, crazy, old woman. She noticed the other cop, Sweeney, had wandered over to the chopping block where she had left her axe. He picked up the axe and held it out before him, appearing to enjoy feeling the heft of it in his gloved hands.

"We've got a search party out looking for her," Mathers went on while Ursula kept a close eye on Sweeney, who began to idly swing the axe back and forth through the air. "She was last seen at the gas station some fifteen miles from here. So, what we're here for, ma'am, is to ask if you have any information that could help us out. You must know these woods pretty well. Seen anything unusual?"

Ursula looked up at Bear Mountain, where the black cloud had grown wider and taller behind the peak and now curved in an arc over the sky.

"Just that weird cloud. How did that happen?"

Mathers looked behind him and glanced at where she pointed. He turned back to face her and shrugged.

"Just weather, I guess. Maybe a storm's coming. I'm pretty sure it's got nothing to do with the missing girl."

"Like I said, I haven't seen anybody. There's no one else out here besides me."

She made to close the door.

"Wait!" Mathers stopped the door with his hand.

Ursula froze. Sweeney dropped the axe on the ground and now watched her with his full attention. Her teeth started chattering despite the mild breeze blowing gently through the open door. She hadn't properly registered what Mathers had said about the missing girl; she was busy wondering about their ulterior motive. She and Bill had waited for something like this to happen for years, some form of government interference. Bill had dealt with cops his whole life: countless times he'd been stopped on the street or pulled over on the road for no good reason. He'd been beaten and arrested for as little as looking at an officer the wrong way. A list of possibilities for why they might be here ran through her head. Not paying taxes; hunting without a license; not having a driver's license or insurance for the truck; or simply because her way of life posed too much of a threat to the status quo. Whatever Mathers said, she knew that cloud was a bad omen. For some reason the hand holding her gun wouldn't move, as though after all this time, after all her preparations, she wouldn't be able to defend herself. Mathers reached into his jacket, and she waited for him to pull out a pair of handcuffs or even another gun, to tell her she was under arrest, but he only took out a card with his name and number.

"If you see anything, you give me a call, okay?" he said, holding out the card.

Ursula took the card between his fingers and held it away from her as though it was a stick of dynamite.

"You're really on your own out here? That must be hard. No grandchildren? No children?"

"Will that be all?"

"Yes, ma'am, that'll be all."

"Watch out for bears," said Ursula.

She slammed the door shut.

Silently, she stayed behind the door and watched them through the spyhole. Mathers turned his back to the door and shook his head. The other cop laughed. She watched while both men got in their car and drove out of sight.

She kept her revolver on her for the rest of the day. There was still a lot of work to do but she couldn't concentrate and only managed half of the tasks she'd planned. She finished skinning the lynx and overcooked the meat on the barbecue. After eating dinner on the sofa, she picked smoky, stringy lynx out of her teeth and drank Last Frontier straight from the bottle while the sun sank. In the fading light, she opened her journal and wrote for a few minutes, trying to capture the significant details of her day, but writing about her intruders – spies building a case against her, no doubt – only quickened her pulse. She gave up when her hand began to cramp, closing the journal and tossing it and her pen onto the cluttered coffee table. Usually, Ursula found writing an exorcism. Via her pen she expelled demons: worries and epiphanies that tormented her during the repetitive practicalities of life off-grid. She'd started keeping a journal after Jake was reported MIA, which helped to fill the long, too-quiet evenings in the cabin; it was a way for her to express thoughts when Bill would barely communicate. She would fill one journal and begin another. By now the books filled four boxes: years of a life captured on paper. Occasionally she picked out an old journal and flicked through it but could not remember writing the words.

Darkness swallowed the last of the sunset. She drank the end of the whiskey and tried to stay awake in case the Aurora Borealis appeared. Eventually the empty bottle slid out of her hand and rolled across the wooden floorboards, where it clanked into another empty bottle lying on its side. She drifted in and out of an uneasy sleep under a pile of Bill's sweaters, hugging her gun, plagued by dreams of sirens and screams.

She saw it the next morning, when she went over to the window to look outside, her hands wrapped around a steaming cup of coffee.

A bear.

Gemma Fairclough*

What looked like a black bear cub, anyway – a small black mound in the distance, lying at the mouth of the forest. One of its legs stretched out across the grey slush of melting snow. It remained still as though it were dead. Sometimes cubs fell from the treetops, or other bears killed them.

Ursula zipped up her coat, tied her boots and went outside. She approached the bear cautiously, holding out her rifle, her boots crunching over dirt and gravel. A bear would be something. Black bear fur was beautifully soft, the meat tender and delicious. The thought of steaks made Ursula's mouth water. She had avoided hunting bears after Bill disappeared – but finding a dead bear almost felt too easy. She had been hoping to put a bullet in its head.

But about twenty yards away, Ursula realised the lumpy black mound wasn't a bear at all. It looked like a balled-up coat. It was covering something. The leg stretched out in the slush wasn't a leg; it was a black sleeve, and at the end of it wasn't a paw but a small, pale hand.

She knew what she'd find the moment she saw the hand – before she knelt down beside the furred body that lay curled up in the foetal position: of course it was the young woman the police were searching for, her cheeks ice-cold and ghost-white, her lips blue. Ursula's first instincts whispered: *Leave her there. Go back inside. Don't get involved. Don't try to help – it's not worth the bother. Let them find her.* But she didn't leave the girl's side. She shook her by the shoulder

113

and rasped, "Hey, can you hear me?" Her voice was like an old motor sputtering back into use.

The girl didn't respond. Ursula repeated herself, wishing her voice wasn't so hoarse from last night's drink. She picked up the girl's arm – the one she had mistaken for a cub's leg – and held two fingers against the wrist. The pulse she found was light and sluggish. She lifted her fingers and saw the shape branded onto the girl's wrist in greenish black ink: a snake eating its own tail, just like Mathers had described.

Ursula noticed something else, too, as she turned the girl over onto her back and her bare legs, which had been curled up to her stomach, slumped down flat on the ground: except for the fur coat wrapped tightly around her, she was naked.

Ursula tried to ignore her racing thoughts and aching knees as she got to her feet, squatted down, and lifted the girl into her arms. *Don't rush*, she told herself, taking care with every footstep back to the cabin, figuring that if she tripped and fell, both of them might be done for. Her trembling arms were beginning to give by the time she got through the front door, and she dropped the girl onto the sofa as gently as she could manage.

She paused to catch her breath and stretch out her arms. The girl's eyes fluttered – as though she'd merely drifted to sleep. Ursula herself was beginning to wonder if this was all a dream, and any minute she'd wake up on the sofa, cradling an empty bottle.

She shook off the thought; there was no time to waste.

There was too much to be done. She sprang back into action – covered the girl with a heap of blankets – threw another log on the fire – rushed to the kitchen to boil water in a pan, mixing in cocoa and sugar. She used to make this extra-sweet drink for Jake when he returned home after a long walk in the woods. She sat beside the girl, lifted the back of her head and held a cup filled with hot cocoa close to her mouth.

The girl groaned.

"Come on, drink," Ursula urged. She tipped the cup gently against the blue lips and nodded with encouragement when they parted.

"That's it..."

The girl managed a few sips. She gave a barely perceptible shake of the head when Ursula tried to give her more. Ursula put the cup down on the table.

"Alright. But you should try to drink the rest. It'll help you feel better."

The girl tried to speak. She had no voice, only breath. She was whispering something; it sounded like 'mother', but Ursula couldn't hear it properly.

"What's that?"

Ursula moved closer and put one ear against the girl's rough, chapped lips and heard them mouth the same word again and again: *bear, bear, bear...* She was drifting back into unconsciousness. Ursula patted her sleeve to try to rouse her and felt how the fur was damp and cold.

"Let's take off that coat," Ursula said.

The girl moaned and shook her head feebly. Ursula carried on, proceeding with what was necessary. She lifted the girl by the shoulders until she was sat upright and then, holding her up with one arm, used her other hand to gently pull the end of one coat sleeve. The girl flinched and yanked her sleeve from Ursula's grip. Her eyes shot open, fixing upon Ursula fiercely.

Ursula would not back down, even under that firm, accusatory glare. "It's soaking wet," she growled. The strength was returning to her voice.

"Don't take off my skin."

Apparently, the girl had found her voice, too – raw and breaking though it was, as if she might have been recovering from the flu, although it was more likely caused by the death grip of cold around her throat. She seemed to summon all that was left of her remaining energy in the effort to form sentences. Ursula heard her accent: definitely British.

"I'm talking about your coat," Ursula said, "it's wet through. You need to take it off so you can get warm and dry." The words sounded strange coming from her: she wasn't used to speaking to anyone at length like this. She wasn't used to speaking to anyone, period. She hadn't had cause to do so all that much, not since the day Bill had vanished into the woods.

"*No*," the girl snarled.

Ursula's heart pounded: she needed to act quickly. But losing her temper would only make things worse. She sighed irritably and pointed to the girl's legs. "What happened to the rest of your clothes?"

"Too hot. Didn't need them."

"That's the hypothermia talking. It plays tricks on you. Makes freezing to death feel like hellfire." Ursula considered the girl for a moment, willing herself to stay calm. She spoke as mildly as she could manage. "We're gonna hang up your coat so it gets nice and dry. Let me find you something to put on in the meantime. You'll feel a whole lot better once you've got the warmth back in you. You can put your coat back on later. I won't take it away. I'll put it right there on that chair by the fire. Okay? Deal?"

The girl glared a moment more before she softened and nodded. She appeared to have exhausted her last reserve of strength. Her head drooped, her chin resting on her collarbone. Her arms slumped to her sides, cool and clammy to the touch when Ursula peeled off the coat. Her scrawny legs were scratched and scraped, as though she'd been running through thorny bushes and thickets.

Why was she running? Ursula pondered this, along with the many other *why* questions running through her mind concerning this girl turning up at her home: *why was she only wearing a fur coat? Why is she here? Why me?* What did Mathers call her again? Jade. If Jade had been running, what had she been running from? Or towards?

Her questions could wait: Jade needed clothes. Ursula decided against lending her own clothes, given how tatty and worn they were. She entered Jake's room – the bed made and ready, everything still in its place, his world map tacked onto the wall, his tape-player and dog-eared copy of *The Lord of the Rings* gathering dust on the nightstand.

In the closet, Jake's shirts and jackets were hung on the rail, his pants and underwear neatly folded on the shelves, and stowed at the bottom were his boots, still flecked with dirt from the last time he wore them. Her hands trembled as she picked out a mauve flannel shirt, a pair of jogging pants, boxer shorts (she briefly faltered, wondering if Jade would mind wearing men's underwear; she shrugged off the thought), vest, socks.

She gathered these up in a bundle and brought them back into the living room, where a wave of warmth hit her and the fire crackled and roared, tall orange flames dancing behind the grate. Jade was lying back on the sofa, wrapped in a towel, gazing at the coat hung over the back of the chair.

Ursula placed the clothes on the edge of the sofa. Jade sat up and surveyed them for a moment, then leaned forward and picked up the boxer shorts, letting the towel slide off her chest. Ursula looked away. She saw that the cup of cocoa on the coffee table was empty.

"You hungry? I'll fix us something."

She left Jade to dress and hurried to the kitchen. For some reason she felt like she was intruding on Jade, not the other way round. As Ursula stirred a pot of lynx stew on the stove, its thick gravy dark brown and bubbling, she wondered why Jade had not yet asked where she was or if she could call her family. Ursula carried two steaming bowls of stew and two spoons back to the living room.

"I don't eat meat," said Jade, gazing blankly at the bowl Ursula held out to her.

"You don't?"

"Never mind. It doesn't matter." Jade took the bowl. She prodded at a lump of meat with her spoon, scooped it up, sniffed and looked at it curiously, then finally took a bite.

"Whereabouts are you from?" asked Ursula, trying to make conversation, mumbling through a mouthful of stew.

Jade shrugged.

Ursula chewed and swallowed, puzzled at why Jade wouldn't divulge this information. People usually liked to give you the boring facts about their lives. Then again, Ursula had never liked to volunteer information about herself, especially not to strangers. She'd never been one for small talk: maybe that's why this was so difficult. She realised she knew Jade's name though Jade had never introduced herself.

"I know who you are," said Ursula. Jade opened her mouth as if she was about to say something, then decided against it. She looked down at her stew and took another spoonful.

"The cops were here yesterday, looking for you. They said you'd gone missing."

Jade didn't answer.

"Want to call them? Let them know you're safe?"

Still no answer.

"Don't you want to go home?"

Jade put the spoon back in her bowl. She looked Ursula straight in the eyes.

"It isn't home anymore," said Jade.

"Runaway, are you?"

Jade looked down again at the bowl in her lap, apparently not wishing to confirm or deny Ursula's guess. Ursula began a different tack.

"What were you doing in the woods?"

"I was looking for something."

"What?"

"Bear."

"You were looking for a *bear*?"

Again, Jade didn't answer. Her eyes shone bright and clear in the flickering flames.

"Have you heard of skinwalkers?" Jade asked.

Ursula was surprised; she had never expected such a question from a stranger. Of course, she had never expected to invite a stranger into her home – a stranger who was, supposedly, missing. This was all wrong. This was trouble. Ursula knew she'd made a mistake. Yet sitting with this girl and speaking of creatures wild and strange while logs popped and crackled in the rumbling fire between them – while time was ending somewhere just beyond the cabin walls – began to thaw a part of Ursula that for too long had been frozen. Unbidden, memories came back: she, Bill and little Jake sitting around the fire and roasting marshmallows, perfuming the air with burnt sugar; Bill telling them stories of skinwalkers and Land Otter Men, of the Wendigo: the forest-dwelling monster who craved the taste of human flesh. Ursula recalled the terror and awe on Jake's face.

Jade misunderstood Ursula's silence. "They're people who can turn into animals. Some do it by wearing an animal's pelt," she elaborated, her cheeks flushing as she spoke.

120

"It's happening to me too. I'm transforming. But I've not finished yet. I need to complete the ritual. I need to find Bear."

"Enough," Ursula snapped. She slammed her bowl down on the table. Things had gone too far. The girl's outburst had drowned out sound of the crackling fire, driven away the memories of Bill and Jake. "You could have died. You can't just wander through these woods with next to nothing on for a spot of bear-watching. Out here, you need to know how to survive."

"I'm not trying to survive."

She's delirious, Ursula told herself, *out of her mind*, but she wasn't so sure. It was certainly odd hearing someone else talk with such conviction. Most of the people Ursula had ever spoken to were filled with uncertainty. If you questioned them about why they went about their lives the way they did, they had no answers. They were shocked and affronted when Ursula asked basic questions of them, such as why they accepted things the way they were. And now, here she was, on the brink of asking Jade that crucial question: *Why?* Only Jade seemed to have an answer ready – not one that would make sense to Ursula, that she was sure of – but, then, Ursula's own answers had never made sense to anyone apart from Bill. Other people thought they were the crazy ones.

Ursula decided upon her words carefully. "You're saying you're trying to change. Or transform. And you don't belong in the place you ran away from," she said.

Jade nodded.

"You don't want the cops to find you."

Jade shook her head.

Ursula sighed. "Okay. Alright. I need to think. You should get some rest."

Jade settled down on the sofa. The flannel shirt was long and baggy on her, like a loose-fitting dress. Ursula came over and covered her with the blankets. Her half-closed eyes were fixed upon the coat drying on the chair.

"I thought I saw something earlier. In the sky," she mumbled, drifting to sleep. "A cloud shaped like a bear. It was eating the world."

Jade slept while the remainder of the day burned away like the logs in the fire. Whatever work Ursula had been planning to do was forgotten: other tasks demanded her attention and obliterated her normal routine.

She collected all the empty bottles littering the living room floor, suddenly noticing what a mess they made lying there, and began washing them, realising they could be reused to store barley and oats. Part way through washing up, however, it occurred to her that the fire needed relighting, and she left the bottles lying in the cooling, cloudy dishwater, forgotten. When dinnertime approached, she found there wasn't much lynx stew left, so she looked in the pantry to see what else was in; the pantry, she discovered, was in chaos. As she restacked the shelves, holding cans up to the light and squinting at their faded labels to see what they were, she wondered how she'd allowed things get into such disorder. Before today, all of this had seemed perfectly normal to Ursula: one day blended into the next as she went about her solitary existence. With another person here, dependent on her for help, an old, familiar sense of duty returned, such as she hadn't felt for a long time. It was an unwelcome feeling. It nagged, bothered, oppressed.

She glanced through the window every few minutes, anxiously watching the road winding around the hills. Thankfully, no cars came. At that very moment, a party of searchers in orange jackets could be out there, discovering Jade's discarded clothing; it was only a matter of time before the police would return. It wasn't Ursula's fault that Jade had turned up outside her home. She'd known nothing about Jade's disappearance before yesterday. But the longer she delayed the call, the worse the consequences might become.

Still, it was against her principles to comply with police. Even if she tried to assist, Ursula suspected they would find fault with her somehow; the government didn't want people like her to walk free. Calling the cops felt akin to snitching: it was clear that the girl did not want to be found. Part of her wanted to keep Jade a secret. Yet the responsibility was grave. While Jade was here, she would never have peace of mind. She took Mathers's card out of her pocket and re-read the number. She and Bill had never installed a phone line, of course – there'd been no one they wanted to call, and they certainly didn't want anyone calling them – but there was a payphone at the gas station to be used in emergencies. She could drive there while Jade was sleeping and be back before she woke up.

Instead, she slumped onto the chair before the fire, bottle of Last Frontier in hand. Outside, it grew dark and shadows began to surround her, falling on the photos of Bill and Jake on the sideboard, on the wolf's head and the glass case housing the eagle. The amber liquid in the bottle caught the light from the embers as Ursula tipped it into her mouth. Jade squirmed and whimpered now and then as she slept, as though she was having a bad dream. Ursula felt the coat on the back of the chair, still damp to the touch.

Glowing green snakes began to writhe across the night sky, their tails lashing through the window into the living room. The wolf blinked, eyes sparked. Saliva dripped from its jaws as it spoke with Bill's voice.

"You shouldn't have taken her in."

"She almost died of hypothermia. I had to do something."

"You did. Now let her go."

"The cops are looking for her."

"Don't call them."

"But they'll come back. I know it."

"They set the trap. Next they'll come back to collect their catch. If you want to help her, set her free."

Ursula shook her head. "They'll find out she was here."

"Not if you send her away first."

She heard the clack of the wolf's teeth; felt its hot, foul breath waft across her face, smelling of its last kill.

"She's dead set on looking for bears," Ursula whispered. "If I let her go, she'll get herself killed."

"If that's what she wants..." The voice trailed off as the

124

spark left the wolf's eyes. Aurora Borealis had whipped her green tail in another direction.

"Come back, Bill, please."

It was no use. The wolf was just a taxidermied head once more. What a hideous thing, it occurred to Ursula now, to hang a creature's head on a wall. For a second, she saw Bill's head hanging there, blood dripping at the neck, a rigor mortis grimace fixed on his face, eyes rolling into the back of his skull. Nausea flooded over her. She ran to the kitchen and stood over the sink, retching, bringing up sour remnants of stew. After she was done, she wiped her mouth on the back of her sleeve and came back into the living room, where the quality of the light had changed: the fire had burned out completely, and where before shadows had roamed like predators in ambush, now the living room was bathed in moonlight. Green flames flickered through the window, across the floor, and over the glass case, where the eagle stretched out its wings, one at a time.

"Jake," said Ursula, approaching the eagle. She rested one hand on the case. "What do you think I should do?"

"You wouldn't like it if I told you."

"You think I should call the police."

"That's what I'd have done."

"You were always a good boy. Always wanted to do the right thing. But you trusted people too much. I used to worry whenever you went to the city, when you hung around with those other boys. And then when you joined the army..." Ursula sighed and looked over at the sofa where Jade slept on, peacefully. "You know, she reminds me a little of you. Stubborn. She left her home and her family behind, too. She doesn't want to be found. I could help her."

"Maybe she needs another kind of help."

"What if something bad happened to her back home? If I call the police and they send her back there, that's on me. But it feels wrong to let her go back out there, into the woods. I can't just let her die."

The eagle cocked its head to one side and repeated her words, questioningly: "You can't 'let' her die?"

"Well – alright, I can't control that. Only God decides when your time's up," she recited: one of her father's sayings that still rang in her head after all this time. She'd been raised as a Baptist by a man who believed that the Bible was the only version of truth. A man who'd rebuffed his daughter's questions with a slap, who couldn't accept her marriage to someone outside her own race: that man's idea of truth had struck her as shallow, limited. Since then, she had learned there were many types of truth. Yes, she had accepted Jesus as her Lord and saviour, but where was he now, at the end of the world? She had no time to wait around for the Second Coming – or, she realised, to repeat her father's aphorisms.

"It seems to me," Ursula went on, "like maybe there's no right and wrong, no good and evil. There are only predators and prey, things eating each other or getting eaten, everything trying to survive until it can't. No sense to it, no significance, it just is what it is. If that's the case, then all you can do is try to live for as long as you can."

"You're afraid of death."

"Death is the bear that lives in the forest and will eat me up someday."

"Can you really protect her from that?"

The lights faded and darkness swallowed the room, and Ursula didn't need to see to know the eagle was just a stuffed carcass again. She pawed her way to the sofa and sat beside Jade, listening to Jade's soft snores until the early hours of the morning. Eventually, Ursula drifted off and dreamed of being chased by an unknown assailant through the trees.

Thus far Ursula's life had involved a sequence of decisions made efficiently and resolutely: once a course of action was settled upon, there was no turning back. When she eloped with Bill, Ursula effectively chose him over her own family, knowing that she'd be dead to her father in becoming, as her father put it, an "Indian's whore". When the two of them settled in the cabin, with no other relatives around (Bill's parents were dead by then; his two older siblings had moved out of state to begin afresh with families of their own) and with no friends to rely upon, they foresaw raising their children and growing old together in this secluded place, practically exiling themselves from society.

Faced with deciding what to do with Jade, however, Ursula was sent into a quandary, all her assurance eroded. She'd always been one to listen to her gut but this time her gut offered no intuition. Even her night-time confidants had given her conflicting advice. She tried to push these doubts to the back of her mind when she was around Jade, whom she treated as both a patient and a guest: she prepared her meals, ran her hot baths, laid out fresh blankets and clean clothes from Jake's wardrobe for her. Jade even allowed Ursula to drag a comb through her long, dark hair, which had matted and tangled itself during her escapade in the forest. It didn't feel right to have Jade continuing to sleep on the sofa when there was a bedroom spare, and so, confusing though it was to offer Jake's room to someone else – let alone have someone else under her roof at all – she provided Jade with a room of her own. She set no specific deadline on the hospitality offered. Although after a few days her restlessness and anxiety grew as her own indecision weighed on her. She went on compulsively looking out of the window to check the road was clear. One evening, she felt like writing in her journal, where she might pin down her conflicting thoughts on the page – but the journal was missing. She couldn't think where she had put it. Her pen had gone AWOL, too. There were so many other things to do and think about, however, that Ursula didn't bother to spend time looking for them.

As Jade began to recover her strength and clarity of mind, she made no further strange utterances as she had done on that first day, although she put on her coat as soon as Ursula allowed that it was fully dried, and thereafter wore it all the time. Her answers to Ursula's questions and offers of food and drink were clipped: *Fine. Yes please. No thanks.* When she was done eating a meal on the sofa she'd slip back to her room and close the door. Sometimes she was so quiet, Ursula peeked through the keyhole to check she was still there: usually she was lying in bed, or sitting up, wearing only her fur.

One morning, while Ursula was cutting wood, Jade came outside, dressed in Jake's clothes and the fur coat. Ursula rested the blade of her axe on the ground, where she'd piled firewood on one side, uncut logs on the other. Jade stalled in the doorway, squinting in the sunlight and shading her eyes with one hand. She hadn't been outside since Ursula had found her unconscious almost two weeks earlier.

"You're wearing Jake's shoes," said Ursula, pointing at Jade's feet. Jade clomped a few steps towards her in the oversized combat boots.

"I found them in the wardrobe," she said, adding, "Sorry." She looked troubled. Ursula was surprised to hear her sound apologetic, after days of so little communication.

"Going somewhere?"

Jade didn't answer, looking suddenly unsteady on her feet, like she might faint. Ursula lunged forwards to lend her arm and led her towards the chopping block, where she made Jade sit down.

"I thought I was feeling better," Jade mumbled.

"Where were you going?"

"Is Jake the boy in your photos?"

Ursula was momentarily lost for words. She'd been waiting on this girl hand and foot and couldn't get a straight answer out of her, and here she was asking Ursula personal questions. Then she remembered this stalling tactic. Jake used to do this with her and Bill all the time, evading their questions by retorting with a cocky curveball question of his own. He was always so secretive: slipping off without a word, not telling her the names of friends he was meeting – although sometimes she saw him with other boys, drove past them when she ran errands in town. She never met any girlfriends; Jake wouldn't talk to her about anything like that. It was as though all that existed for him outside the cabin went on in another world, far away from her and Bill. Jake always found a cunning way to deflect the topic of conversation back onto her.

She studied the young face now watching her with that same mixture of earnestness and deceit. For some reason it amused her, struck her fondly. "Yes, that's Jake," she replied, smiling in spite of her frustration.

"You were talking to him. A few nights ago."

Ursula thought back to her conversation with the eagle – one she thought had been private – and felt abashed. "You heard that? I thought you were sleeping."

Jade, on the other hand, did not appear embarrassed, self-conscious or afraid to admit to eavesdropping. Instead, she seemed to consider Ursula thoughtfully, as though trying to make sense of something.

"I wondered if it had been a dream," she said. "There was so much green light."

They looked at each other for a moment, an understanding forming between them. Some of the colour had returned to Jade's cheeks. A cloud passed overhead and the harsh sun drained away so that everything became softer, the cabin and the dirt beneath them and the piles of wood all in gentle sandy hues. Jade got to her feet.

"Come on, help me with the wood," suggested Ursula, placing a log vertically on the block. "I'll show you how to split it."

"I know how to do it."

Ursula offered her the axe and watched with surprise at the confidence with which Jade lifted it and drove the blade through the log in one stroke. The two halves fell apart on the ground, their insides clean and smooth.

"Where did you learn how to do that?" Ursula laughed.

Jade smiled, not giving anything away. Ursula knew what she was thinking: it didn't matter. Whoever she had been didn't matter anymore. That's exactly what Ursula had decided for herself when she had been about Jade's age, when her whole family had turned their backs on her, when she and Bill began their lives off-grid. She found a new way to live. Maybe that's why Jade had come here – to find another way of being.

"There are other things I could teach you," said Ursula. "When you're feeling a little better, I could take you hunting. Do you know how to fire a gun?"

"I think I need to lie down," said Jade, her colour drained again. Ursula admonished herself: she'd pushed the girl too far. She ought to be more patient. She put her arm around Jade and helped her back to her room, where she tucked her under the bedcovers. On the nightstand, she noticed, was the journal and pen. She was about to say something, but Jade was already asleep. Her first impulse was to snatch the journal away; its contents were private. Her charge's breach of her privacy was, on account of Ursula's principles, unacceptable. Then again, she had sacrificed her privacy the morning she brought Jade into her home. It had been reckless to leave her journals lying around – even to write them in the first place – when they could easily fall into the wrong hands. But were these hands, now burrowed beneath the pillow where Jade's head rested, capable of doing Ursula wrong?

Jade slept on peacefully, strands of her long black hair draped across her face; Ursula found herself stroking these away, gently. Perhaps Jade's taking of her journal – not stealing, given that she'd made no apparent efforts to conceal that she'd taken it – was an act of tender curiosity, born of a sincere, innocent desire to learn more about her host. Or maybe Jade intended to continue writing in the journal herself, which would help to fill the long, quiet days of her recovery. That suggested Jade was comfortable here – settled. Ursula left the journal and pen untouched, stood up and left the room.

Every now and then, Ursula came back to check on her. She checked the road: all clear. It was strange the cops had not been back yet. Still, Ursula thought, searching for a missing girl out here would be like looking for a needle in a haystack – perhaps they'd already given up. That night, instead of slumping on the sofa with a drink, she lay fresh sheets on her and Bill's bed and, once she lay down, fell asleep within seconds.

The bathroom light was out. The bulb was fine, the filament still intact, so she tried switching on lights in other rooms.

None lit. And her chest freezer, filled with cuts of meat, had no power.

She inspected the solar panels, which were fine, and which should have absorbed enough light yesterday. Then she checked the generator. The battery was dead. There had to be a spare somewhere. She searched through the cabin, through all the boxes piled up in the living room and her and Bill's room (how had she accumulated so much junk?); she turned the place upside down and still couldn't find another battery. She'd have to go to the store.

She looked in on Jade, who was still asleep. It would take about an hour to drive to the store, pick up a battery and some other supplies, and come back. When Jade was very sick, Ursula had avoided leaving her alone in the cabin for longer than half an hour in case she needed anything, going no further than the edge of the forest to collect her quarry from the nearest traps. Now Ursula faced another problem. Jake's boots lay on the floor at the foot of the bed where Jade had kicked them off the day before. She was growing stronger – growing restless. When she woke up, she might try to go out again. Without Ursula around to watch over her, she might wander into the woods and get herself lost – or worse. Although Jade hadn't said anything quite so strange as she had on that first day in her hypothermic delirium, Ursula hadn't forgotten what she'd said about looking for bears. If a skilled huntsman like Bill could vanish during a bear hunt, a novice like Jade stood no chance. And there were more than bears to worry about: the woods could devise a thousand ways to kill you.

It's the right thing to do, Ursula assured herself, though her hands shook as she slipped the key into the lock on Jake's door. It went against her instincts – after all, who was she to control another person? But she had to intervene; Jade's life was at stake. Ursula also had to admit – pathetic though it was, given that for years she'd managed perfectly fine on her own – she dreaded returning to an empty house. First Jake had left, then Bill. Somehow she had learned to cope over the years, found pleasure in small things: the scratch of her pen on the pages of her journal; ensnaring animals on her trapline; biting into meat she had caught and cooked by and for herself. She had grown to enjoy the quiet and solitude of the cabin, her love-hate relationship with the brooding forest and nothing else. Since Jade's arrival and all the attendant responsibilities of this, however, she remembered how much of her life used to revolve around family. She and Bill may have rejected society and embraced the wilderness, but they always assumed they'd have each other – until Ursula had no one. Once again she had another person to think about, to look out for, to do what was best for her. It was hard, it was stressful – but it had begun to shape her life again. An old scar she thought long healed over was cut open and gushing bright red blood. She didn't know how she'd be able to stop the bleeding if she had to go back to living without another soul. She wouldn't even have her nocturnal visitors anymore with Aurora Borealis season ending. The prospect of getting used to being alone in that cabin all over again was too much. She turned the key gently until she heard the soft click of the catch.

Most likely she'd be back in time before Jade woke up, and she would unlock the door and Jade would never know. If Jade woke up, of course she'd be angry, but Ursula would explain how she'd never meant to frighten her; she'd only ever tried to protect her.

The drive took longer than expected. There was a traffic jam on Bower Road; someone had hit a moose. On the road ahead that bended to the right, she could make out the curve of its antlers, its bulk a dark heap on the tarmac, its legs sprawled at unnatural angles. A full-grown male, looking at the size of it. Parked beside a ditch at the side of the road was the damaged car, a huge dent in its hood. She couldn't see the driver. A couple of men got out of their vehicles and went over to help: they bent down either side of the moose, lifted two legs each, and began to drag it towards the ditch.

Ursula tapped a frantic rhythm on her steering wheel. *Come on, come on...* she muttered under her breath, watching them grow red-faced as they struggled under the moose's weight, having barely moved it a few yards. In her rear-view mirror she saw a police car approaching behind her. Her stomach flipped, even though she knew they were only here because of the road accident – weren't they? This was the fourth police car she'd seen since she'd set off. When the officer got out and started speaking to the men hauling the moose, Ursula gave up and did a U-turn, doubling back and taking another route along Totem Avenue.

Ten minutes later, she passed another police car and thought she recognised Mathers at the wheel. There was even another guy in the car wearing earflaps, like the other cop had worn when they accosted her that day. The way the driver stared straight at her before turning into the road she was just leaving bothered her too – if it was Mathers, he'd surely have recognised her, recognised the truck. They'd probably made a note of her long-expired license plate when they came by her house that day and couldn't wait for a chance to catch her driving on public roads and arrest her.

She felt dizzy, short of breath. When the car was out of sight, she did another U-turn and stepped on the gas. The store would have to wait. She'd manage without the battery – after all, she'd trained herself to be prepared for privation at whatever point the rest of the world lost power and was thrown into chaos. The birch trees crowding both sides of the road became a ghostly blur of green and white, disappearing when she turned into the narrow mountain pass. She wound her way back along the bulges and recesses of the mountain, passing a yellow AVALANCHES warning sign, feeling a dead weight in her chest as though rocks and ice had already cascaded on top of her. An enormous shadow passed first over the valley, then the road ahead: it was cast by that strange and now muzzle-shaped black cloud.

She could tell that something was wrong even as she glimpsed the cabin from a distance. Speeding up the long driveway, she flicked the windshield wipers on, just in case it was only debris obstructing her view – but as she screeched to a halt, she saw that she was not mistaken. Jake's bedroom window had been smashed. A breeze lifted a corner of curtain through the frame.

She got out of the truck and hurried over to the broken window, ignoring her aching back and knees. Then she saw the blood. Droplets, some as large as nickels, dotted the ground amid sparkling shards of glass; a train of them ran underneath the window along the front of the cabin and across the clearing. Ursula followed the blood until it disappeared at the mouth of the forest. In spite of all the animals she'd butchered over the years without a trace of squeamishness, the sight of the blood now made her dizzy. It had traced a fault line across her small, peaceful corner of the earth: her world seemed like it would tremble and break up any moment. Without stopping, without thinking, she ran across the vegetable patch to the well, drew a pail of water, came back and threw the water over the blood. She kept going until the last of the red trail had washed away.

She turned and went back to the cabin. It should have been impossible for Jade to get out of her room; inconceivable that she, a slip of a thing in a weakened state, could break through reinforced glass. Ursula leaned in through the gap where the window had been – noticing a bloody smear on the frame, which she hastily wiped away – and shouted Jade's name, even though she could see it was useless: Jade wasn't there.

A fragment of glass jutting out of the frame caught one of her gloved hands: it tore through leather and skin, yet she didn't feel pain. She let herself in through the front door and tried the door to Jake's bedroom, which was still locked. She unlocked it and looked inside once again. The room was a mess of broken glass, shreds of fabric, paper and fur, but there was no one inside. Aside from Ursula's ragged breathing, the cabin was silent. She closed her fist tight against the warm wetness gathering in her sliced palm and searched every room, calling Jade's name over and over. There was no answer.

Eventually she found herself back in the living room, staring back-and-forth at the wolf and eagle. "Where did she go?" she repeated aloud. Both stayed silent. Neither flinched nor looked back at her. Were they mocking her? Punishing her for having made the wrong choice? At a time when she needed them most – but no, Bill and Jake would never have subjected her to that. For all their faults, they had loved her. These creatures couldn't be her husband and son after all. It had only ever been a trick of the light. These beings were alien, indifferent: her concerns were not theirs. She, Bill and Jake may have made possessions of the bodies of animals, but there was something behind the eyes they could never capture. Once they fired the gun it was extinguished forever. So it had been when she had finally found Bill's remains: a heap of meat and rags left in the woods. It was better that Jake and Bill were gone – better that they weren't trapped here with Ursula, fighting to survive. There was relief in knowing, now, they were free; terror in realising they'd left her utterly alone. Here she stood among dead things, unseen, unheard. If a woman falls in a forest and no one is around to hear her, does she make a sound?

She took her rifle from the gun rack, planning the clear-est route through the forest, the way Jade was most likely to have taken. That's where the blood had led to: the forest. Jade couldn't have gone far; Ursula would surely find her, rescue her again, take her home. If Jade had fled, it was because of a misunderstanding. With time, Ursula would be forgiven, and then she needn't spend her last days alone. They could co-exist quite well, Ursula was sure: she could teach Jade how to survive and how to forget everything that had come before. They would live out their lives here, unknown and unknowable to the rest of humanity, like almost all life on earth.

A dark shape stirred in her peripheral vision. She looked through the window. At the mouth of the forest – in the exact same spot she had noticed Jade on that morning two weeks ago – stood an enormous black bear. Ursula thought it must be the alpha male, judging by its size. It seemed to be watching the cabin, waiting. She slowly opened the front door and went out, creeping alongside the cabin, making no sudden movements. The bear didn't move. It just watched. Ursula steeled herself as she cocked her rifle: she was sure the sound would provoke the bear. It flexed its huge front paws and snarled: it seemed to know what she was think-ing, what she was planning to do as she aimed her gun at its head. The two of them stayed like that for a time: how long, Ursula could not say. Time slowed. They stayed still as a photograph: the two of them facing each other, Ursu-la's gun aimed, her finger on the trigger. Then she noticed the strands of long, dark hair caught in the bear's muzzle, blowing in the breeze.

The scream that came out of her – for it surely couldn't have been her own voice – must have carried across the mountains, it was so loud and piercing and terrible. It would ring in her ears for weeks afterwards, wake her from her nightmares, chime with the metallic noise of prison gates closing and locks turning. It was like nothing she'd ever heard, yet if pushed to describe it, she would say it was like the screech an eagle makes as a bullet bursts its wing.

Before, time had slowed to a crawl; suddenly, it sped up into a sequence of blinks. A crack of gunfire. Bear growling, recoiling. She'd missed. Hair dangling from its teeth. Aiming again. Bear retreating into the mouth of the forest. Another, different growl: the noise of tyres churning gravel. Looking up: a police car approaching, coming for her.

Aiming the gun.

Epilogue

"This isn't a good town," Ursula reminded me when she began her story.

Not that I needed reminding. My family moved to Fairbanks for several months when I was seventeen, and at the time I solemnly believed they did so just to punish me. Now I appreciate my parents had reasons of their own: my father had been out of work for nearly a year after being laid off from his teaching position at Portland State (budget cuts had gutted the English department). My mother, a history professor, was the sole breadwinner until her health took a turn for the worse, forcing her to cut down her hours and, eventually, to quit her job. Somehow my father heard about the temporary teaching vacancy for a Creative Writing summer school programme at the University of Alaska Fairbanks and, perhaps envisaging a bucolic haven far away from the pedestrian disappointments that had befallen us in Portland, decided that the upheaval to a new home in another state was just what we all needed. That spring in 1997, when I had just finished my junior year of high school, I thought my failing grades had prompted my parents' decision to take me away from my friends and the city I'd known all my life and dump us in this middle-of-nowhere, purgatorial place in uber-conservative Alaska.

The only thing that impressed me was the scenery. For the whole summer, while still furious with my parents – themselves even crankier than usual from lack of sleep thanks to Alaska's midnight sun – I went out hiking every day in my Doc Martens, keen to explore this extreme, gorgeous landscape. On one occasion I filled my backpack with supplies and camped out for the night, not returning until noon the next day, giving both of my parents another sleepless night and near-coronaries. They forbade me from taking camping gear out of the house after that: another entry to the ever-growing list of 'forbidden' activities, which also included hitchhiking and using a fake ID to get into bars. Still, I was pretty much left to my own devices that summer – my father was busy with his new job and my mother had decided to finally sit down and write a book. My parents were obviously as clueless about Alaskan life as me, having no idea that hiking in the summer carried the highest risk of encountering bears; if they'd been aware, they might never have let me leave the house.

Usually on my hikes I met no one else but the occasional moose, fox or lynx. Pickup trucks drove by every so often. Otherwise, I was left to the landscape: the sublime heights and sudden drops of the mountains; giant, ancient trees whose roots snaked through miles of earth; the roaring, ever-churning Tanana River and her whispering tributaries. One day I went through a forest, curious to climb Bear Mountain, which I'd spotted on my map. After an hour of walking, however, I still couldn't find the mountain trail.

Whichever direction I turned there was only more spruce and fir, their fallen needles blanketing the forest floor and dampening the sound of my increasingly hurried footsteps: had I come this way already? Was I going in circles? Where was the way out, anyway? I may as well have been in unchartered territory. I crumpled up my map and flung it into the dirt.

I was peering through the trees for some hint of a clearing or a road, when I saw something move between them, approaching in my direction: a teenage boy. He hopped over the thick, gnarled roots protruding from the dirt without having to watch his step, as though he knew their pattern so intimately he didn't need to look down. I stood still and waited for him to notice me. He glanced at me and looked away, quickening his stride as he passed me by. His apparent desire to get away from me made me instinctively trust him. He wasn't like the boys I knew from home, cocky and self-assured, who would have called out to me: "Hey, you. What's a girl doing out here on her own?"

So, I called out to him. He stopped dead in his tracks. "Can you help me?" I asked. Another item checked on my parents' 'forbidden' list: talking to strangers.

He seemed to hesitate before sidling over. "You're not from around here," he said. He watched me as warily as a deer. There was something strange, almost otherworldly about him. He seemed to have come out of nowhere, simply materialising from the trees: a spirit of the woods.

"One hundred percent certified townie, that's me," I said. "Nice to meet you. I'm Carla."

"I'm Jake," he replied.

He was over six feet tall, muscular and lean, and yet there was a boyish smoothness and softness in his face. I liked the coy half-smile that broke out over it as I took his hand and shook it; he seemed amused by my introduction.

He guided me through the woods while I chattered on without pausing for breath, without giving him time to give complete answers to the series of questions I rattled off about Fairbanks: what exactly are you supposed to do around here? Was it true even the eight-year-olds carried guns? Is there really a town called North Pole nearby which celebrates Christmas all year round? Jake listened and laughed, politely offering a correction or an alternative view when he could get a word in edgewise. (Ironically, the adult-me is now required to spend most of my time listening to other people telling their stories: the raw material of my writing.)

We agreed to meet for another hike the following day, and again the day after. We slipped effortlessly into friendship, the way kids do. I did the bulk of the talking. I was used to shouting and interrupting just to be heard; back home, everything – friendships, school – was built around competition, fighting for popularity, for the top spot. Next would be college. I told Jake I had no intention of studying hard at school, or applying to the Ivies as my parents wished, for no reason other than you were expected to compete – it was all bullshit anyway. I waited for Jake to agree but he offered no opinion, so I continued talking while he listened. He didn't appear to mind my yammering, the way I anticipated silences and filled them. I was flattered by his attentiveness, which seemed genuine and free of ulterior motive. I was used to boys only drawing me into conversation for one reason, and even then they barely listened; for that reason, along with having no interest in dating boys, I didn't have many male friends. By comparison, Jake's companionship – which felt mature, fraternal, respectful – surprised and soothed me.

I learned about Jake in snippets, on the rare occasions he volunteered scraps of information about himself. I was curious to know more but sensed I shouldn't push. I gathered that he didn't have any other friends. The few local boys he used to play ball or wrestle with as little kids had moved on to video games and pot. He didn't understand their references, their TV shows and music tastes, how they interpreted someone's choice of car or haircut or clothing within their complicated social hierarchies; they didn't get him, the shy, homeschooled kid whose parents were crazy survivalists. They were looking forward to finishing school and getting jobs or applying to college, even moving out of state – meanwhile Jake would continue living at home, working with his parents in the fur trade. Still, he'd see them around from time to time, and they'd get along okay. Things weren't too bad until the rumours started.

"What rumours?" I blurted out after Jake mentioned this – apparently by mistake, as he looked mortified, which only piqued my curiosity more. It discomfits me now how much I pressed him, although at the time I thought I was being a good listener and confidante. I assured him I'd keep whatever it was a secret. By this point I'd told him some secrets of my own: that I was missing my girlfriend back home in Portland; that I had come out to a few friends but still hadn't come out to my parents.

Eventually, he gave further details, averting my gaze as he did so. There'd been one boy he'd been particularly close to – a boy who didn't mind explaining the cultural references Jake missed, who didn't ask probing questions about whether Jake's parents were conspiracy theorists, Mormons, or alien-hunters. For a while they saw each other nearly every night after the boy finished school, slipping away to hike together on the mountains.

"One day we were best friends," Jake said, "and, literally, the next he wouldn't speak to me. Wouldn't even look me in the eye."

"But why?" For once, I was quiet, hanging on Jake's every word. I pictured Jake and this mystery boy alone together on the mountain peak – holding hands, perhaps, or sharing a kiss as the Northern Lights painted the sky green.

Jake didn't elaborate. He skipped over that part of the story to a few weeks later, when he went into a diner in College and saw a group of boys – including his friend – sitting together in a booth. The moment they saw Jake they got up and left the booth. As they exited the diner, a couple of them shot hostile glances that told Jake everything he needed to know. The boy he'd been best friends with called him a filthy word: one of several words that would continue to follow him around when he drove to the store or made a delivery; words that would be whispered or sniggered or stammered,

angrily. Those words haunted and taunted him like polter-
geists wherever he went.

"What did they call you?" I asked, although I could have
guessed. For some reason I wanted him to spell it out for
me, and I was impatient to hear it.

Jake shrugged. His cheeks had reddened; though he
smirked as if the whole thing was stupid, I could see he was
blinking back tears.

I rolled my eyes and sighed, launching into what I
assumed would be a helpful speech: "There's nothing wrong
with being a 'queer' or a 'fag' or whatever it is those douche-
bags call you. They're the ones with a problem. I also had a
'friend' at school who started a rumour about me, and *she*
was the one who kissed *me* first..."

Here I proceeded energetically with my story and filled
the silence that might have otherwise fallen firmly between
us. I even managed to make him laugh. He wiped his eyes.
He seemed relieved – or that's how I saw it at the time; I'll
never know for certain how he felt. The conversation turned
to other topics. I told him I dreaded going back to school
in the fall, I had no idea what I'd do next. I don't think it
ever crossed my mind to ask Jake about his future plans. If
it bothered him, he didn't show it. He looked at me thoughtfully and said: "You're a good storyteller. I think that's what
you should do."

I'd like to say our friendship lasted. But, inevitably, it
was a summer thing: when my father's contract ended
and we were packed up and ready to head back to Oregon
(my father had got another job there and my mother had

secured a book deal), I promised I'd write to Jake and mail my letters to the PO Box he'd given me. I'm ashamed to say I never sent a single letter. School started and I was back in the city with my friends, back to a full social calendar. Fall became winter and I still didn't know how to start, what to write. The summer seemed so long ago.

When I visited her in jail, Ursula didn't want to talk, didn't care about my desire to exonerate her. She didn't trust me, and why should she? She looked at me the same way she looked at the jurors and law enforcement officers and lawyers and reporters during her trial: she looked through me. She grunted in response to my initial greeting and ice-breaker questions, sighed and chewed her nails as I introduced myself. She had little to say at all until I told her about the boy I'd met in the summer of 1997. The boy whose photograph I had noticed on a TV documentary's footage of the inside of her cabin, twenty years later.

From that moment her whole aspect changed. She looked at me in pure wonder, astounded as I described that boy, his appearance, his manner, the hiking routes he led me through and knew so well.

"That's him, that's my Jake!" she cried.

She was hungry for details. I told her about the view of the waterfall from Bear Mountain where Jake had taken me, held a finger to his lips, and pointed to the gorge below: I counted seven bears standing firm in the river, unswayed by the water's force. The bears waited, their attention fixed on the frothing torrents, until a salmon leapt above the surface – with a quick, calculated turn of its head, one of the bears caught the salmon in its jaws. Jake had laughed, watching my amazement; I had never seen a bear in real life before that day.

"What did Jake say?" Ursula kept asking. Or: "What did he do then?"

She was surprised when I told her that Jake had wanted to travel. I remember being surprised too, when he told me: I had taken him for someone who couldn't imagine a world outside his small town, beyond the forest and the mountains.

"Where did he want to go?"

"He wasn't specific. I think he just wanted to see what else was out there." I hesitated before what I said next: "I guess that's why he joined the army. To see the world."

I waited for Ursula to lash out at me. Instead, she looked pensive. "I never knew that," she said. "I just thought it was about duty. Patriotism."

"Maybe it gave him a sense of community as well?"

Ursula nodded thoughtfully. She seemed much calmer, much sweeter than I'd expected; nothing like the haggard woman on my TV screen who'd lumbered, handcuffed, across the courtroom to the counsel table, where she'd slumped to her seat, head down.

"I think..." I began, watching closely for Ursula's reaction. "Jake was afraid to open up about himself. To tell anyone he was gay."

Ursula stared at me. "He was?"

All her hard edges seemed suddenly to blunt: the cold and spiky assuredness that had helped her get through the trial and her conviction and jail abandoned her, and only a frail old woman was left.

"He would never talk to me about... about that kind of thing," she muttered.

"It's a hard thing to talk to your parents about."

"You knew him better than me after one summer, when I had him for twenty-three years."

After that, I got her to tell me her story over the course of several visits. In general, she seemed to be glad of the company. If she fell quiet and needed encouragement, I would tell her about another time I'd been with Jake, what we'd talked about and in particular what he'd said (if only I'd let him say more), filling silences just like I used to.

There are many gaps in Ursula's story that, perhaps, warrant exegesis. I shall leave it up to readers to speculate about the veracity of her account, to consider how her version of events sits alongside the revelations we find in Jade's thesis, and ultimately to judge for themselves whether she deserved to be convicted for Jade's murder. There is one detail in Ursula's story which I believe holds the answer to her exoneration, if only the riddle could be solved: that is, the cause of the broken window in Jake's bedroom.

Witnesses, police detectives and forensic experts offer differing viewpoints of how the window was broken. Most agree that the breakage occurred in the period between Ursula locking Jade inside the bedroom and the arrival of Mathers and Sweeney. During Ursula's trial, police detective Nick Corvid, who arrived at the scene shortly after the shootout, testified that the broken window "appeared to be the sign of a struggle" that took place during this period, yet under cross-examination could not confirm that it pointed to a struggle between Ursula and Jade: there simply wasn't evidence to verify this.[16] Nevertheless, at this point in the trial, the media frenzy following Ursula's shooting of Mathers would have been fresh in the jurors' minds, and this is likely to have made it difficult for them to imagine a struggle without picturing Ursula as the aggressor. Even if there had been a physical struggle between the two women, it was hard to see how this could have produced the kind of intense force needed to shatter the reinforced window. One ballistics expert familiar with the case, whom I contacted for comment, proposed that a bullet fired at close range could have shattered the glass. In their view, since there was no reason for Ursula to shoot her own window from outside, Sweeney must have fired a stray shot that hit the window. This theory, diverting from the generally accepted timeline that the window was broken before the police shootout, seems unlikely: first, because both Ursula and Sweeney claimed that the window was already broken when the two Troopers arrived at the scene (and Sweeney insisted he fired only one shot). Second, because although broken glass was discovered both inside the bedroom and outside beneath the window – making the direction of the fracturing blow more difficult to call – more shards were

---

16 See transcripts from court proceedings on the Alaska Trial Court Cases index, *Ursula Smith v State of Alaska*.

found outside, indicating that the window was most likely broken from inside the house, and therefore not from a shot fired from outside. Third, because no bullets or shrapnel were found in the bedroom, indicating that something other than a bullet shattered the window.

Another theory is that Jade smashed through the window in order to escape the locked bedroom. Forensic expert Jane Steiner, who was called as a witness by the defence during Ursula's trial, pointed out the higher number of glass fragments found outside the window make it likely that the fracturing blow or pressure was applied from inside. Had Jade been incapable of breaking the window with her own hands, as Ursula believed, then she would have had to use a gun or some other means to break it. Perhaps Jade stole a firearm from Ursula's gun rack and sneaked it into the bedroom before Ursula locked her in.

There may even have been another person who arrived at the scene before Ursula returned home from her drive. Perhaps a passing hiker heard a woman's screams coming from the cabin and, understanding she had been locked in, tried to help. A resourceful individual might have found various objects around the property they could use to break a window, such as a tree branch or Ursula's axe. After helping Jade escape, the passer-by could have made the decision not to get any more involved and simply gone on their way. Not everyone chooses to come forward with important information during an investigation of a missing person, so great is the worry of appearing suspicious, even if they're innocent. Of course, it's possible that if another person had smashed the window, their intentions weren't so innocent. According to Ursula, a trail of Jade's blood led from the window (before Ursula washed it away in a state of shock): whether Jade cut herself while escaping through broken glass as she fled to the woods, or if an assailant dragged her there, is unknown. It's certainly possible that police overlooked other suspects in their rush to charge Ursula with Jade's murder. With Alaska's high prevalence of violent crimes committed by men upon women,[17] even seemingly innocent bystanders ought to have been considered. Why, for example, was Jade's partner not a person of interest, when he arrived in Fairbanks on April 16, ostensibly to assist with search efforts for Jade, and stayed in the area for the next month? Given his close (and, as we glean from Jade's thesis, troubled) relationship with Jade, surely even a man police described as "fully cooperative" should have been probed and questioned further.[18]

It's also not unheard of for bears to break into homes in Alaska, often in the search for food. Ursula claimed to

17 See "Alaska ranked most dangerous state for women and girls", *Alaskan Herald*, September 19, 2020.

18 During a press conference following initial police investigations of Ursula's property, a reporter asked Fairbanks Police Department spokesman Peter Franklin-James if the police were looking into any other suspects involved in Jade's disappearance, adding, rather bluntly, that current or former partners were often suspects in such cases. The spokesman replied: "We're not looking into any other suspects at this time. Jade's partner was still in England when she was reported missing on April 15. He subsequently travelled to the area to assist voluntary search parties and has been fully cooperative with the police." See "Police shooter Ursula Smith prime suspect in British woman's disappearance," *Fairbanks Daily News-Miner*, May 18, 2016.

have seen a bear on her property shortly before the police arrived (which Sweeney didn't corroborate, although driving uphill towards the cabin would not have provided the necessary vantage point to view the bear in the location Ursula claimed to have seen it). A small amount of bear fur was discovered inside Jake's bedroom, although this could have been brought in indirectly, for example, on Ursula's boots after a hunt. If a large bear was determined to get into that room, it would probably have been strong enough to break in. This might explain why glass shards were found both inside and outside the room: perhaps the bear broke in through the window, entered the room, then shook out its fur as it exited, leaving more glass shards outside the window than remained inside the room. Although bear attacks on humans are rare occurrences, there have been other cases of bears breaking into homes and attacking, even eating, their inhabitants. If this theory seems farfetched, members of certain online forums assert an even more extraordinary theory: that Jade, trapped inside the bedroom, transformed into a bear, broke out through the window and escaped to the forest in her animal form.

The most significant question of all is Jade's current location.

Most likely, and most tragically, Jade has died. If Ursula or some other malefactor didn't kill Jade – if, after all, there never was a wolf in grandmother's clothing – other dangers lurk in the forest. Most of these are invisible. The extreme cold alone poses a significant threat to one who is unfamiliar with and unprepared for surviving harsh climates. Other potential risks for someone as ill-equipped as Jade include starvation and malnutrition. If she did manage to escape the cabin and run to the woods, bleeding, it's almost certain she carried no medical supplies for treating wounds. The most optimistic view is that she survives, as yet untraced, in the largely uninhabited Interior region. Lost to the wilderness, she may never be found.

While Jade's disappearance has struck terror into the hearts of some, for others it has become inspirational. Ever since her thesis was leaked online and subsequently disappeared, acquiring even greater notoriety as a result, Jade has become (in)famous among the therian community. Belonging to the broader otherkin community – a subculture of people who identify as non-human – therians (also known as a therianthropes) are people who identify as nonhuman animals. Many therians report experiencing "shifts" into their animal identities, which are usually acknowledged to be spiritual or psychological, as opposed to physical. Therians are distinct from better-known furries: people mainly interested in anthropomorphic creatures (i.e., animal characters with human-like qualities) who often express their "fursonas" through online avatars, dressing up, roleplay or art. The therian community is largely made up of young people living in affluent nations in Western Europe and in the US, but it also has a significant presence in other countries including South Korea and Japan, making it global and heterogeneous. As with all subcultures, among therians there are factions and splinter groups, several of which have developed a significant following only recently. For example, therianthropy has taken on a radical political undercurrent for some: these therians generally follow politically liberal and progressive causes, attributing their shifts into animal identities to their rejection of heteronormative, capitalist ideology (though there are notable examples on the far-right of the political spectrum, such as the English Bulldogs, a community of nationalists who envisage shifting into dogs in order to protect their national borders). The majority of therians, however, agree on one point: that their shifts into animal identities do not involve any physical shape-shifting, and they understand that they are physically human; in their view, Jade's story has fuelled misconceptions about therianthropy. However, a small yet growing group seek literal transformations into their animal identities, with some imbibing psychoactive drugs to induce a more 'animal-like' state or even undergoing surgery to transform themselves physically. Among this latter group in particular, Jade's thesis has struck a chord; many of its members, whose online spaces and social media profiles continue to proliferate the viral #iamjade #bearseason trend, perceive Jade's disappearance not as a cautionary tale but as a model example.

There have been disturbing cases of individuals following in Jade's footsteps: journeying to Interior Alaska, or other remote locations inhabited by bears, with the intention of becoming bears themselves. In most cases these individuals have been found unharmed and rescued. However, the disappearance of nineteen-year-old Bernadine Woods, who stole her mother's credit card to pay for a flight from London Heathrow and has not been seen since she landed in Fairbanks, Alaska, in July 2023, is deeply concerning. Her final Instagram post included the #bearseason hashtag, a clear homage to Jade's legacy.

Jade is gone for now, but not forgotten. Let no stone go unturned; ensure no mistakes are repeated in the search for Bernadine Woods: the investigation may shed light on more than one mystery. Meanwhile, a generation of disillusioned young people seek alternative possibilities, other ways of being.

Transformations are underway.

APPENDIX

Abstract submitted by Jade Hunter for consideration for the 4th Global Symposium on Fairy Tales, Fables and Folklore on November 30, 2015:

Beast, lover, doppelgänger: the bear and its relationship to women in fairy tales and folklore

Friendly and fearsome; maternal and violent; godlike and monstrous: the bear has embodied all of these seemingly antithetical qualities in fairy tales and folklore across the Northern Hemisphere. Ambivalent literary representation of bears may be a cultural response borne from practical concerns in places where humans have lived in close physical proximity to these animals. Bears frequently command authority in stories from the oral traditions of Indigenous peoples in Western Canada and the U.S.A., such as in "The Woman Who Married a Bear", in which bears outwit, reprimand and educate ignorant humans who fail to show them the respect they deserve. In this story, bears also have the power to assume human guises, and by the end, the titular woman gains the ability to transform herself into ursine form.

159

Elsewhere, bears still populate the cultural imagination. One of the most famous fairy tales in the English language is "Goldilocks and the Three Bears", in which bears uncannily mirror human behaviour, eating porridge from bowls, sitting in chairs and sleeping in beds, subverting and blurring the human/animal dichotomy. A girl (or old woman, as in the original version, "The Story of the Three Bears") invades the bears' home to steal food and take refuge, assuming an animal-like status. No harm ultimately befalls Goldilocks when the bears discover her sleeping in their cub's bed, yet the story retains a subtle threat. In *The Uses of Enchantment* (1976), Bruno Bettelheim shows that a sense of menace is typical of the fairy tale genre, through which our fears and issues of identity are conveyed: for example, in "Snow-White and Rose-Red", a tale featuring a benign bear looked after by two girls, beastly behaviours are displaced onto other characters (in this case, a bad-tempered man), which the girls must struggle to overcome.

In these stories, bears and women may be companions or lovers, doubles, or even shape-shifters of each other. This paper will consider the parallels or close relationships the stories draw between bears and women, asking what the bear is, what the woman is and where the line between them – if there is one – falls.

Acknowledgements

First, I'd like to thank Wild Hunt Books powerhouse, Ariell Cacciola, for believing in and publishing my work. I've massively appreciated her publishing wisdom, which has reassured me throughout the process, and her thoughtful editorial suggestions and changes. She is the mastermind behind the successful Kickstarter campaign to fund *Bear Season*'s publication (along with *The Burning Child of Bantry* by Hanna Nielson), in addition to the book editing, production, promotion, sales, and more besides. I'm also hugely grateful to Amy Douglas at Wild Hunt Books, as well as to the other creatives who worked with the publisher, including Laura Jones-Rivera for the typesetting, and Luísa Dias for designing the beautiful cover.

I'm indebted to the women in my writing group, without whom *Bear Season* wouldn't exist. From providing invaluable feedback on sections of the book, to providing ongoing motivation and encouragement, they've helped me to keep writing since 2019. Thank you Sarah Mosedale, Abby Ledger-Lomas, Jane Claire Bradley, Sophie Hanson, Rosie Garland, Janelle Hardacre, Debz Butler, and Summer Meadow Phillips.

I want to thank my parents, Lesley and Vince, for their

enormous support of my education and interests. My multital-ented and endlessly generous mum inspired me to do creative things; I cherish my memories of her love. From my utterly dependable and conscientious dad, I've learned self-discipline, which a writer needs, as well as the importance of taking worthwhile risks, without which I might not have dared to seek publication. He's also one of *Bear Season*'s biggest pro-moters and ought to consider embarking on a new career as a book publicist (he won't; retirement's awesome).

I also want to thank Mel and Alan for championing the lifelong benefits of a love of learning and the arts. Thank you, Mel, for supporting me in myriad ways leading up to the publication of this book – not least with taking breaks with me to chat and chain-drink cups of tea.

I'm grateful to all my family and friends who've helped me along the way, including by pledging towards the fund-raising campaign to publish *Bear Season* and/or spreading the word to others. Special thanks to my aunties Collette and Clare and to my dear friends: James, Rachel, Amy, Laura, Sonja, Holly, Nat, Farina, and Sarah.

Thank you to my lovely colleagues at Manchester Met-ropolitan University who cheered me on and pledged sup-port for *Bear Season*'s publication.

Finally, to Dave, who was always there – literally, in the same room (it was a small flat) – while I wrote this book; who read many drafts and offered thoughtful feedback; who made countless brews and meals to allow me more time to write; who gave me love and support every day: thank you for everything.

Author Bio

Gemma Fairclough is a writer living in Manchester. She has a BA (Hons) in English Literature and a Master's in Contemporary Literature and Culture from the University of Manchester. She recently completed the Write Like a Grrrl programme and formed a writing group with peers from the course. A range of unsettling influences, including horror films, surrealist art, and folklore inspire her writing, which frequently centres upon experiences of alienation, grief, and aberrant desire.

Twitter @GemFairclough

Wild Hunt Books would like to thank the following
Lifetime Supporters:

Daniel Sorabji

Jan Penovich

Blaise Cacciola

If you're interested in becoming a supporter,
please contact us at info@wildhuntbooks.co.uk